The Wind's Kiss

Julia Lindesay

FOR ANDY

Because I wouldn't have done any of it without you

PROLOGUE

It was a hellishly hot morning in the middle of the Australian desert. The sun burned and the warm breeze provided no relief as I looked up at the massive rock towering over me. Its intense red contrasted with the blue sky in a scene of ancient natural beauty. I glanced back at the carpark packed with people and vehicles, the only sign of civilisation in the vast desert wilderness.

In my rush to get here, I hadn't grabbed sunblock or a hat, but I couldn't turn back now. Cherie was depending on me to save her from a crazy, power-hungry demigod. Sunburn was the least of my worries. I took a deep breath and started walking before fear could keep me paralysed at the foot of the giant sandstone rock - Uluru. The name echoed in my mind as I heard it spoken in a tone of awe by a tourist walking near me.

The path around the base of the rock was wide, well-formed, and packed with people. I passed harassed parents with small children complaining loudly about walking in the heat, older couples, trim backpackers speaking German and a busload of Asian tourists. I longed for someone, anyone, to notice me and help stave off the sense of loneliness creeping over me and weakening my resolve. No-one even looked my way, even though I pushed past them murmuring apologies.

I soon reached the point where people were hauling themselves up the steep side of Uluru, holding tightly onto a chain, ignoring the several signs asking visitors not to climb the rock. Anger stirred in me at the crowds determined to climb the rock before it was finally closed out of respect for Australia's First Nations people in a few months' time. No doubt today's rare solar eclipse was an added drawcard.

The receptionist at my hotel in Alice Springs had told me that people sometimes fall off the side of the rock or die of heart attacks. I was afraid of what would happen to me today. Although my own heart was beating fast, whatever happened to me out here wouldn't be as mundane as a heart attack. I welcomed the anger as it burned away some of the anxiety.

I left the rock climbers behind me and continued around the base of Uluru for over an hour, focussing on the ground beneath my feet and letting the wild beauty of the place seep into me and bring me calm. Mind-blowing rock formations and enticing crevices tempted me to stop and look closer, but I stayed focussed on my purpose. By the time I reached the far side of Uluru, the heat had slowed me considerably and I was sweating like crazy.

All the tourists who had been walking the trail with me had turned back to avoid being out during the worst heat of the day and I was now truly alone. My feet hurt, the traumatic experiences of the past weeks weighed on me and I was afraid I wasn't going to be where I needed to be before the eclipse at midmorning.

A horrible cry sounded behind me – like a cross between a strangled cat and a wounded horse.

I froze, fear churning in my stomach. I didn't want to turn and look because I knew what I'd see. If only I'd never gone to that stupid dance party Cherie would be safe now and I'd be tucked up with a good book on the window seat in my bedroom. But I knew that wasn't true. Nothing could have prevented me being here today, alone and afraid, with only hope to lean on.

1 AN ATTACK AT THE FIESTA DEL SOL

It was Cherie who dragged me to the Fiesta del Sol, the hottest dance party of the year. Waiheke High School had just ended for seven weeks of holidays and the endless round of summer parties had begun.

"Chad asked after you at Hone's beach party last night," Cherie said as she lounged in the window seat of my bedroom.

I was relieved I'd missed the party if Chad and his friends were there. Since Chad left school three years ago, he had done nothing except grow his hair long, wax his surfboard and inspire all the girls at school to moon after him. In fairness, there were a lot of awesome beaches on Waiheke Island and being a beach bum was a tempting lifestyle if you had no ambitions.

"So, tonight there's no backing out" Cherie continued. "You only turn seventeen once, babe! If you won't let me throw you a party, we have to do something. Or are you going to stay here with your mum instead, and dance around that ridiculous fence post in the garden?"

"It's a *maypole*, Cherie, not a fence post and that's what you do at summer solstice. Besides, how many beach parties can I go to in a row? Mum needed me to work at the Frying Fish last night." I paced the room, staring out the window at Mum directing Dad as he put the maypole up in the middle of our overgrown lawn. The long, bright ribbons fluttered in the breeze and my baby brother squirmed in Mum's arms, trying to catch one.

Cherie rolled her eyes. "Seriously? You want to stay and dance around the post…" She rose from her seat.

I sighed and turned away from the tranquil garden scene. "I guess not. Look, I'm getting ready now."

I knew the Fiesta del Sol was not to be missed. People came from all over the mainland to our small island for it, and here I was living just ten minutes away. I rummaged in my closet for more party-friendly clothes than the t-shirt I'd worn to work at my parents' fish 'n' chips shop. Cherie settled back in the window seat and gave unsolicited advice on my clothing options. She was already dressed to impress in a slinky white top and tight black pants. I finally settled on high waisted denim shorts, a flowing white top, boots, and a feather necklace. This received a tacit nod of approval from Cherie as appropriate Fiesta ware and ten minutes later, I waved to my family in the garden as we headed to the bus stop.

"…and I really want to see Nick D." Cherie was prattling on about the festival line-up as we stood waiting on the grass verge. "Are you listening, Jasmine?"

"Um … sure, Cherie, I think Nick D's pretty sick too." I had zoned out thinking about the book Mum had got me for my birthday. It would have to wait.

"Hmmm," Cherie muttered. She carried on cheerfully talking about the festival until the bus pulled up. Tina was already onboard and beckoned us over to seats she and her twin Josh had saved for us.

"Kia ora kōrua! Glad you decided to come, Jas." Tina gave me a sunny smile. "Happy birthday. We got you a present, but it's back at our house. Come by tomorrow and get it."

"Of course, she came! The lure of Chad is too much for

her to resist," Cherie responded.

I glared at her. "Per-lease! I'm sure he prefers voluptuous blonds like Cherie, not scrawny mousy-haired types like me." I opened the window to let in some air and my hateful fine hair flew into my mouth.

"Your hair isn't mousy, Jas. It's definitely auburn with hints of red." Tina pushed her own wild dark hair away from her face as the wind reached her too.

"Don't underrate yourself," Josh chimed in. "A lot of guys would be keen on you if you gave them the chance."

I looked away, uncomfortable under Josh's gaze and irritated that he would make up something like that. Luckily, Cherie was distracted by a guy from school behind us and was soon deep in animated conversation. Tina talked about the music line-up as the bus cruised along the narrow bush-lined laneways of the island to the vineyard hosting the Fiesta del Sol.

The sun was setting as we got off the bus and the neat rows of grapevines crawling over the slopes in front of us were backlit by a dying golden light. I let the beauty of the scene seep into me and felt glad that Cherie had convinced me to come. A spark of excitement lit in me as we wandered down the red dirt driveway to the natural amphitheatre amongst the vines. A warm-up band was on the stage, the musicians inciting the crowd to wave their arms in the air and move their hips slowly to their mellow beats. I smiled as I recognised one of my favourite local bands.

I started to head towards the stage, but Cherie grabbed my arm and hauled me over to a group at the edge of the crowd. I saw with a feeling of dread that Chad was amongst them. Tina shot me a sympathetic look as we left her and Josh behind.

"Hey Chad, whassup?" Cherie tossed her hair and overemphasised her words as she accepted a joint from a skinny woman next to her who I'd never seen before.

"Cherie, babe. Just chillaxing ... Hey, this is your friend Jasmine, right?"

I suppressed a shudder as he embraced us both even though I had never even said hello to him before. He reeked of alcohol, and I stepped back as soon as I could.

"Hey," I replied, looking back at Josh and Tina. Tina was focussed on the music, but Josh winked and pulled a face before turning back to the stage. I tried to sidle away and engage in the music, but Chad put an arm around me again and pulled me away from the others. He was too strong for me to resist without making a scene and nobody noticed us go, not even Cherie who was holding three guys in thrall with her conversation.

Up close, Chad's blonde dreads were smelly, and his face was scarred by acne. Without all that, he could have been cute. Once.

"If I told you that you had a beautiful body, would you hold it against me?" he whispered in my ear, stroking my face with his nicotine-stained fingers.

Yuck. "Er, pardon. Hey, look, I should get back to my friends." I tried to push away from him.

He evidently thought we'd talked enough already and launched himself at me. His mouth crashed into mine, he grasped me around the chest and dragged me with him, out of sight of the music festival and deep down a row of vines.

"Mmm." He pulled away briefly to gaze intently at my face. "Sweet-smelling Jasmine, just as he said."

"What ... who said what?!" I gasped, "Just get off…"

But he was all over me again and now I was afraid. He crushed me against him, hands roving all over me. He wasn't taking no for an answer and was clearly too drunk to be sensible. Anger replaced fear as I realised this – partly at myself for not creating a scene before now, and for letting him drag me out of sight of everybody. The sun had completely set, and it was completely dark, with only faint starlight above us and an even fainter glow through the grapevine leaves from the direction of the stage. The music was loud even this far from the stage, and no one would hear me if I screamed for help.

"What part of no don't you understand, you creep?" I fought, hitting him on his back and the side of his head, but he was too close for me to put any power into it.

He batted me off and tried to push me to the ground. "Relax, babe. I know you're green, but you and me, we're meant to be."

I managed to spin us both around and hook my foot behind his ankle. He fell backwards and pulled me down on top of him. We landed awkwardly on the grapevines and the ripe scent of squashed grapes filled my nose. I leaped up instantly and turned to run but was stopped by a loud cry.

"What the hell!"

I couldn't see what Chad was yelling about at first. He was flailing on the ground in a panic, tangled in the vines. Then I saw it. A grapevine was slithering around his torso and pinning him to the ground.

"Oh my God," I shrieked in an embarrassingly high-pitched voice, but only Chad was around to hear, and he was busy. Then I fainted. I collapsed to the ground and the world went away.

2 THINGS GET STRANGE AND SCARY

"Are you okay?"

I opened my eyes to see a young guy leaning over me. I could just make out his coffee-coloured eyes and brown hair in the soft light of a torch he was holding. For a long moment I couldn't work out where I was or why I was afraid, and then the memory of Chad's assault hit me. In a panic I tried to get away from the guy with the light, but I could only scrabble weakly at the ground. The stranger held out his hands as if to calm a wild animal and stepped back.

"Hey, hey, it's okay. I'm not going to hurt you." He sat down cross-legged and waited for me to relax.

I struggled to a sitting position and clutched my knees to my chest. My body complained at the exertion, and I almost blacked out again. I was unbelievably thirsty, and my tongue was stuck to the top of my mouth.

"Still pretty out of it? Don't worry, you'll be alright soon. It hits all of us this hard when we first use the Earth's energy." He was talking nonsense, but with a lovely accent: American with a hint of Latino.

"The vines grabbed Chad! How did that happen? Where is he?" I shivered at the memory. Fear crawled up my spine and nestled in my throat and I couldn't stop breathing in short panicky bursts.

"It's okay." The stranger's voice was calm. He cautiously stepped towards me and put his hand on my arm stroking it gently. "You must have felt threatened by something and the vines responded to your call for help."

"What?" Maybe I was hallucinating this guy. He wasn't making sense, and he certainly wasn't from around here. What a shame; he was kind and his touch on my arm had driven away what could have become a full-blown freak-out. I looked around. Chad was gone, a tangle of vines lying on the ground where he had been. Maybe I had hallucinated all of that too…

"It must be an experimental grape variety they have growing here."

The stranger smiled as if I'd made a joke and held out a hand to help me up. I took it and felt its solidness in my hand. Not a hallucination. My sight blurred a bit again as I stood up but steadied after a few moments. Close up, the stranger smelled nice, like a forest in the rain; damp earth, cedar and pine. I started shivering and felt my breath quicken again, but not in fear this time.

"Here." He handed me a thermos from the backpack slung on his shoulder. "Drink this – it will help."

I gave him a dubious look. We'd all heard stories of girls being drugged in bars by strangers giving them drinks.

Understanding dawned in his eyes and he took a swig himself before offering it again. I was so thirsty, I stopped worrying and took a long steady drink. It was warm and minty with hints of lemon, but it also had flavours I'd never experienced before – earthy and chocolatey but deeper and richer somehow. I sighed as I drained the thermos and shook my head, at once feeling much stronger and more like myself.

"What is this stuff?" I handed him back the thermos.

Before he could answer I heard someone call my name.

"Jasmine!" Tina, closely followed by Cherie and Josh, appeared out of the vines from the direction of the concert.

"Where have you been? The festival's nearly over. We've been texting you for ages!"

"Huh." I looked around and tried to get my bearings in the darkness. The only light came from the light carried by the stranger and strobe lighting from the distant festival stage.

My friends surrounded me, all talking at once. The stranger pressed his torch into my hand and stepped back. The torch's light died as soon as my hand closed around it, and we were all plunged into gloom.

"You dropped this" he said, and I could only assume he was talking about the torch he had put in my hand. "I'll see you again, Jasmine."

"Wait! I don't even know your name," I called after him, trying to push past my friends. Despite my relief at seeing them, I wished them anywhere else as the strange self-assured teenager vanished into the vines. He didn't pause or even look back, so I turned to my friends with no idea what to tell them about what had happened. I could barely sort it out in my own head, let alone provide a coherent and believable explanation to someone else.

"I'm not sure what happened. I think I had a bad trip on something Chad gave me ... and he kind of attacked me."

"But you never take drugs," Josh protested. "What did he do to you? Where is that creep anyway, I'll ..."

"Oh, forget it, he's not worth it." I didn't want Josh to get into a fight with Chad who was strong and clearly unhinged. "Look, I'm really tired. Can we just leave it for now and get out of here?"

Cherie and Josh both insisted I tell them exactly what had happened, but for once Tina talked over them.

"Leave it, you guys. I think she needs to go home and rest now. Tomorrow morning we'll take her to Uncle Duncan to report the attack — the police should really handle this." She looked meaningfully at her twin.

I wasn't sure I had the nerve to report the attack and its

confusing aftermath to anyone, even Tina and Josh's friendly uncle, Waiheke's only police officer. Still, I was relieved when everyone agreed with Tina's plan, and I could focus on getting home to my cosy bed. I was also grateful for Cherie's steadying arm as we stumbled in the dark, feeling our way back down the row of grapevines to the main festival area. From there we went straight up the lamp lit driveway to the buses. Despite the revitalising drink, I still felt unsteady and wiped out; as if I had just finished a marathon. Josh and Tina came behind us, arguing quietly about what to do about Chad.

"At least tell me who that hot guy we found you with was and what that thing is that he gave you?" Cherie looked at the torch still clutched in my hand.

"I don't know. Just some guy who helped me." I didn't want to talk about the stranger until I'd had a chance to process everything myself.

Cherie raised her eyebrow. "Just some guy, huh? He was so hot!!"

I looked at her warily. "You thought Chad was hot, too." I only meant to deflect talk from my rescuer, but I couldn't keep a note of accusation out of my voice.

"Oh hey, I am sooo sorry about Chad. I never would have tried to set you up if I knew what a creep he was." She looked genuinely confused. "In fact, I don't even know why I was trying to set you up. He's really not your type at all."

"It's alright, Cherie. It's not your fault. Just don't try and set me up with anyone else. Okay?"

Cherie grimaced and nodded.

I had a quick look at the object in my hand as we walked. I had thought it was a torch, but now saw that it was a light grey oval shape with two perfectly flat surfaces – it would make an amazing skipping stone and had the same texture as a rock. It was smooth and warm and fit my hand perfectly. Maybe there was a switch on it somewhere to turn the light on. I put it in my jeans pocket to examine later, away from prying eyes.

There were plenty of buses waiting out by the road, as the musical festival had not quite ended. We got on one that was nearly full, and it soon left, heading for Oneroa, Waiheke's main centre, and the ferry terminal. The night air was warm, and the bus quickly became stuffy, sapping everyone's energy after an evening of dancing. Still, some people looked like they were just getting going, and there was talk about catching the last ferry into the city on the mainland to find another party.

I was so tired that the thought of partying made me shudder. I closed my eyes for a moment and settled back into the seat. I was gripped by the memory of Chad leering over me, and I opened my eyes again in distress. I'd just experienced my first kiss and it was not at all how I'd imagined. I decided not to count this one and call it what it was; an assault. I firmly banished Chad from my mind and allowed my eyes to close again. I must have nodded off, lulled by the rocking of the bus, because I jolted awake suddenly when it came to a stop and the engine noise died.

Through the window I saw that we'd come to the end of the bus route at the ferry terminal. People brushed past me laughing and calling to each other as they got off the bus. My pocket with the torch in it was hot and making my hip ache. Cherie, Tina and Josh had also fallen asleep and were only just waking up. I groaned in quiet despair, thinking of the long uphill walk from the ferry terminal to home.

"Gah." Josh made funny noises as he woke "Weird. I never nap in buses, or anywhere else."

"Me neither," said Cherie.

"Well, it is pretty stuffy." I shifted my legs and unstuck my sweaty thighs from the vinyl seat. I'm always nodding off in all kinds of circumstances so there were no alarm bells ringing in my head. That is, until the driver came down the back of the bus and stared at us. He didn't look like the driver that we'd got on the bus with. He looked like a monster from a gothic horror movie!

I looked around to see if anyone else had noticed, but

only the four of us were left on the bus. Cherie gripped my arm tightly as the lights inside the bus went out. I could no longer see the driver's face, except for his eyes, which glowed a sickly green in the dark. He loomed over us, his head brushed the ceiling. A beard that looked like it was made of grass and vines was sprouting from his chin, falling as fast as water to his navel. He lurched towards us with a horrible cry – a cross between a strangled cat and a wounded horse.

Tina screamed. Josh yelled, "Move it!" and we all moved, tripping over each other in the dark, towards the back door of the bus which was mercifully open.

Cherie stumbled down the steps after me and I hauled her up. The driver (or whatever it was) came after us. His gait was stiff as if his knees didn't bend, but he wasn't slow. Since the bus was parked across the ferry terminal entrance, blocking the exit to the road, we ran onto the wharf.

"The ferry," gasped Cherie and we all pelted towards it.

The wharf was well lit, and we could see the ferry workers at the end untying the boat and pulling the gangplank up. Terror fuelled our feet.

"Wait for us. Please!" I yelled at the ferry attendants.

They didn't wait. They never do. We made it anyway, leaping in quick succession from the upward sloping ramp and over a railing onto the deck as the ferry pulled away.

"Hey, you kids!" one of the wharf side attendants shouted. "You know better than that."

I stared past him down the wharf but could no longer see the bus driver.

"Forget it, Jack," muttered the attendant next to him, "we know who their parents are."

"There was something chasing us," I yelled back at them, partly to warn them and partly to excuse our behaviour.

They both gave us dirty looks as the ferry pulled away. We watched the wharf until we couldn't see it anymore as we tried to catch sight of the monster that was chasing us. Nothing appeared, so we headed inside the empty passenger cabin. All the other passengers – mostly kids like us who'd been at the Fiesta del Sol – had gone up on the top deck to enjoy the balmy evening air.

"What the heck was that?" Tina said as we sat on the hard, plastic chairs. Her hands were shaking as she leaned on Josh. "It was like a freaking monster or something ... or was it just someone in a costume?"

Josh and I exchanged glances and he jerked his head towards the ferry's small bar. Josh was a believer in the restorative powers of a cup of tea.

"I'll get one." My own hands were shaking as I slipped out of my seat. There was only one staff member at the bar, who appeared to be closing for the night. Even in my anxious state I noticed that he was new and way younger than most of the late-night bar crew usually were. I took the ferry so often that I knew all the faces, and a lot of the names, of the crew.

He was gorgeous. Yes, two gorgeous strangers in one night! He was lean and tall, with an angular face and a prominent nose, but the imperfections only added to his appeal. Fair hair fell to his shoulders, and his piercing blue eyes were looking straight past me at Tina.

With something like a smirk, he said to me, "What's up with your friend? She looks like she's seen a ghost."

He had a soft voice, his accent a cross between those of the Scandinavian and British tourists who enjoyed Waiheke Island each summer. I smiled weakly and tried not to ogle him. I was tempted to tell him about the bus driver-monster, but caution stopped me.

"Just a run in with her ex," I said. "You know how it is. A cup of tea would help her feel better if you aren't already closed?" I looked at the sparkling clean bench and cabinet.

He shrugged and reached for a cup. "I don't think I'd like to run into her ex. You all look like you've been chased by a monster."

I stared at him but couldn't bring myself to respond. He turned and busied himself making the tea. Maybe he had seen the bus driver chasing us.

Handing me the tea, he smiled at me properly; a cool and wild sort of smile that promised all kinds of things. Terror gripped me all over again, but for a completely different reason. His smile turned amused as he reached behind my ear and produced a flower, like a cheap magician. He offered it to me. Feeling my face redden, I snatched the flower and fled back to my friends before he could see.

The others hadn't even noticed my interaction with the bartender. Cherie was jiggling her foot and rubbing Tina's back, which made it hard to focus on her words as she gave us her theory.

"Look, he was probably just some guy in a spooky costume playing a trick on us. I think we overreacted. Anyway, there's no point in speculating."

I could see from Josh and Tina's faces that there had been plenty of speculation in the short time I'd been gone.

"I have a plan," she continued.

Cherie always had a plan. I groaned and exchanged a grimace with Josh.

"We'll follow everyone else to whatever club they're going to and party on till dawn. Forget it happened. If anything else weird goes on …well, there's safety in numbers."

I sighed. Cherie's plan sucked. I was exhausted and strung out before we were chased by a monster. I was ready to collapse.

"That plan sucks, Cherie." Josh spoke up before I could. "Jas looks dead on her feet and Tina's not in the mood for partying."

"Sorry Cherie, but Josh is right," I added.

"Jas!" Cherie's tone changed. "Where did those flowers in your hair come from?"

"What?" I reached up.

My hand touched a mass of flowers, stalks, and leaves – practically a bush. I pulled at it, and a bunch of flowers came away with a stab of pain, as if I'd pulled my hair out.

It was giving off a sweet, delicious scent, which I recognised as the weedy but pretty plant that had taken over parts of our garden: night-blooming jasmine. I looked at the flower the bartender gave me. It was the same. Cherie started to clear the plant out of my hair with sharp tugs.

"Ow. Stop, Cherie, that hurts! That bartender must have done this."

I looked over at the bar, but he was nowhere to be seen.

"Feels like it's attached to your head somehow." Cherie carried on tugging, ignoring my protests.

Tina shrieked, and my hair was forgotten as we all turned to see what had alarmed her. It was the bus driver, looking almost normal, apart from a faint glow in his eyes and a horrible grin that spread when he saw us. How he'd made it onto the ferry we'll never know, but he was dripping wet. He stalked past the empty seats towards us. We stared, frozen in shock. Well, except for Cherie. She leaped up and strode towards the driver with a fierce expression.

"Listen, you creep. I don't know what kind of tricks you pulled back there, but we aren't impressed. What the hell do you want anyway?"

She let out a cry as the driver grabbed her and threw her over his shoulder, then strode out onto the deck.

"Cherie!" I leaped up and ran after them, Josh close behind.

The deck along the side of the ferry was narrow, just one step from the inside to the railing. We were well away from the lights of the ferry terminal, deep into the open stretch of water between the island and the sheltering harbour of Auckland city. The driver was trying to throw Cherie over the side into the dark waters below. She was shrieking abuse and snatching at anything she could.

Before we could reach them, he flung her over the railing. She grabbed at it and clung on with both hands, shouting at the driver the whole time. Distracted by our arrival, he turned away from her and lurched straight towards me. Josh pushed me aside and leaped on him, but the driver was strong and threw him straight off. Then the driver turned and picked me up as if I was a doll. I screamed and punched at his arms and shoulders, but nothing stopped him carrying me to the side of the boat, just as Cherie hauled herself back on board. The driver tossed me over the railing as if I were an empty beer can. Unlike Cherie I did not manage to grab the railing.

It was a long way down and I hit head-first. The impact and the cold water took my breath away. I couldn't tell which way was up or down as the ferry's wake churned around me. My fingers tugged at my boot laces and my greatest regret in the world right then was that I'd double knotted them. A tight pain grew in my chest. I fought not to open my mouth and breathe in seawater. Terror added strength to my desperate efforts to reach the surface, but my boots might as well have been concrete weights. I sank deeper and the lights from the ferry faded away and left me in darkness. My lungs were bursting, and I was filled with pure icy horror as the black depths claimed me.

3 A STRANGER SAVES ME FROM DROWNING

Just as I gave into my fate and stopped fighting, someone grabbed my arm and dragged me up through the water. The pressure on my chest was still immense until I broke the surface. I gasped frantically for breath, gulping in great lungfuls of air. Adrenalin coursed through me and I sobbed in relief. I was alive!

"You're okay now, take it easy," my rescuer murmured in my ear.

In the dark I could only see the outline of the person holding me, but I recognised the distinctive accent of the bartender. The guy I had fled from in embarrassment with a red face and flowers in my hair, just minutes ago. My body spasmed as I coughed and gagged, seawater foaming from my mouth and nose. I would sink again if he let me go, dragged back down by my clothes and shoes, and my heavy body. I had no idea how the bartender was managing to keep us both afloat.

Everything went hazy then and the next thing I was aware of, I was on the back deck of the ferry. The hard surface of the deck was beneath me, and the bartender was close enough to kiss me. I wondered if he had been doing CPR on me, but I hadn't stopped breathing completely ... had I?

"It's all right, Petal. You're okay now." The bartender was speaking to me in soft tones, and it was having the intended effect. My muscles began to relax and tension left me. The terror of nearly drowning receded, not forgotten, but locked away in the back of my mind for now.

"Jas!" A voice shrieked. Cherie elbowed the bartender aside and he moved away with the amused smirk he'd worn earlier.

I ignored her, looking straight at the bartender. "Don't ... call ... me Petal!" I managed to choke out. That hadn't been the first thing I intended to say, but it was too late to take it back now. Thank you, or cheers for the rescue, would have been a bit cooler. Irrational as it was, I hated that I had just been rescued. I thought of myself as a capable person, and certainly no damsel in distress. And yet, twice this evening I'd needed rescuing!

Cherie's eyes flicked between the bartender and me and a smile tugged at the corners of her lips in amusement. "Looks like you'll be just fine, Jas."

Quietly she added, "Don't worry, your hero also dealt with the creepy bus driver. I'll explain later."

I looked around. A small crowd had gathered on deck. People from the bus earlier that night and all the ferry crew. Probably everyone on the boat except the guy steering. I groaned, embarrassed to be seen in such a state.

Josh and Tina detached from the crowd and rushed over, exclaiming about my bad luck falling off the boat. My three friends embraced me in a hug that shielded me from the crowd. I welcomed *their* rescue, sagging against Tina and Cherie as they supported me to a seat inside the cabin. A crew member was shooing the crowd away, vigorously, and effectively. I sighed, revelling in the sheer relief of being alive and being blessed with awesome friends.

As for my mysterious rescuer, I expected him to

disappear as the guy in the vineyard had done, but he was standing next to Cherie with his arms folded, giving me his smirk. Somehow, he managed to look good even in his sodden ferry crew polo shirt and plain shorts, an unflattering outfit for anyone at the best of times.

An older crew member sat down next to me, frowning. "We need to get you to the hospital as soon as we dock in case you've inhaled some water. I'll call an ambulance now and have it meet us." I recognised him as the ferry captain and suspected I should know his name.

"I'll sort it out, Captain, don't worry," the bartender said.

The older guy looked like he was going to disagree, but then he glanced at the fast-approaching lights of the city.

"New, aren't you – what's your name again? Indigo? Given your incredible rescue of this young lady tonight, I'm sure you're capable of getting her to an ambulance. I'm going to have a nightmare explaining this to the police when we dock, not to mention your dad, Jasmine." The captain looked like he wanted to grill me on the spot but fortunately he didn't have time before we reached the city.

Now I remembered, the captain's name was Harry, and he was a windsurfing buddy of Dad's. He asked me several quick questions to make sure I was still with it and checked my vitals. With a final warning to be more careful next time, he rushed off to the ferry's bridge.

Cherie, Tina, and Josh were deep in conversation with Indigo. What a lovely name, I thought as I let my eyes close for a moment. Lulled by my friends' voices, exhausted from a stressful and eventful night, I fell asleep on the vinyl cushion seats reserved for pregnant women and old people.

*****

I awoke to a sunlit room with high ceilings. I lay sprawled in a large comfortable bed with an amazing view of the city from floor-to-ceiling windows that surrounded me on three sides. The sheets felt silkier than any I had ever experienced and the whole place was light and airy and reeked of luxury. The bed and a plump armchair were the only furniture in the room. I sat up and saw that this was a mezzanine area, open to a void, with a ladder the only exit. My waking brain took all this in without alarm, until the events of the night came back, and agitation grew in me. I patted my hair and was relieved to find that at least there were no flowers in it.

"Arak!" A piercing noise drew my attention to the corner of the mezzanine furthest from the ladder. Right near the ceiling was a huge bird on a perch. It looked like an eagle and had gorgeous golden-brown plumage with black wingtips. It gave me a piercing look, assessing me. I smiled tentatively in response. The bird opened its beak wide and made a high-pitched chattering sound.

There was something familiar about the bird and I was reassured to think it had been there all night watching over me. My agitation was subsiding to a manageable level, chased away by the bird's presence. I wondered what kind of person usually slept here, with a giant eagle in their bedroom.

I slipped my feet out onto a plush cream rug and was disconcerted to see that I was only wearing a white t-shirt and my underpants. I dreaded to think who had seen me in these undies. I had made them myself one year in home economics class out of several different scraps of colourful material. The t-shirt was not mine and smelled like sunshine and salty ocean breezes. I looked up at the bird, to see it staring out the window intently. On the armchair my clothes lay folded up neatly, clean and dry. I dressed quickly, shy of the bird in the corner for no reason I could define and headed for the ladder. I needed to find my friends and discover what had happened to the bus driver last night.

I nodded goodbye to the bird as I descended the ladder. The first thing I saw in the living room below were my three friends asleep on comfortable-looking sofas and bean bags in a large conversation pit. I sighed in relief. It was most likely Tina or Cherie who had undressed me.

From a glance outside, I guessed that we were high up in an apartment building in the central city. The living room flowed into an open-plan kitchen and dining area, and across the room was a closed door from behind which came angry voices.

I stepped closer, my bare feet silent on the thick beige carpet. I don't normally listen at doors, but I needed to know what was going on.

"You've broken the rules already, Indigo. You are always breaking the rules, and this is the *one* time when we cannot afford your games. You gave her the Wind's Kiss!" A man with a similar accent to Indigo's was speaking. He sounded like someone used to having people do exactly what he told them to.

"What was I supposed to do, Father! Let her drown? Then everything would be lost … everything!" Indigo replied.

"Yes, yes, you are right of course … but still, the Wind's Kiss! It is a lot to explain to the Aerie. And then to bring her here – that was foolish and unnecessary. There will be consequences. The Earth Guardians will not let this go."

"Who cares what they think? No one counted on Orlando trying to kill her. He might try again, so I didn't think it was safe to send her to the hospital."

"We don't know it was Orlando," his father interrupted sharply, with fear in his voice. "He hasn't been seen for years."

"But we know he has used leshys in the past and he has reason to want us to fail…"

"Quiet!" The note of command in his father's voice stopped Indigo in his tracks and there was silence.

I suspected I was about to be busted, even though I hadn't made the slightest noise. I started to creep away. Not quick enough. The door was flung open and an older version of Indigo stepped through, followed by Indigo himself. The older man gave me a piercing, angry look. I stared back, giving no ground. After a minute of this silent scrutiny, his face abruptly changed.

"You must be Jasmine. Indigo has told me about you." His smile was sunny. "And who are all these young people scattered around my living room – your friends?" He cast his now benevolent gaze over my friends who were slowly waking at the sound of his voice.

"So lovely to have you to stay. It's always nice to meet Indigo's friends. You must be hungry after your eventful night. Indigo, why don't you take them to one of your favourite cafés. But please come right back as we can't be late for...for our meeting." He retreated quickly behind the door, leaving Indigo alone in the living room with us. Indigo sighed as he visibly struggled to let go of the anger his father had triggered in him.

Tina rushed over and gave me a long hug. I tried not to cling to her when she finally let go.

"Are you okay, Jas?" she asked.

I could only nod because I wasn't okay, and any other answer might have opened the floodgates.

Tina didn't look convinced but joined Cherie in trying to straighten herself out and gather up her things. Josh was the only one unconcerned by bed hair and bedraggled clothes. Although Indigo's dad had already gone, Cherie called after him.

"Hang on a minute. Who are you guys anyway? I saw the way Indigo dealt with that monster last night and the police at the ferry terminal and I want some answers."

I wanted to know what had happened with the bus driver and the police, too, but Indigo had already taken my arm and was ushering me out of the apartment. I was a little bit buttery under his long slender fingers and couldn't see any reason to resist. Cherie and the others had no choice but to follow us as we took the elevator down to the ground floor.

"As I told you last night, I can't answer that," Indigo said to Cherie, without looking in the least bit sorry. He still looked unhappy, but he was calm now. "I'd love to explain everything to you, but I can't right now."

He refused to say more except to comment on what a nice day it was, and how quiet it was in the normally vibrant lane. I looked around, taking it in. I rarely came to this part of the city; in fact, I rarely left Waiheke Island. I found myself ogling the designer clothes in the lane's boutique shops and admiring the small public squares with their artworks and water features.

Cherie and Josh gave up pelting Indigo with questions as he steered us into a funky little café on the corner of one of these squares. He finally let go of my arm as we sat on comfortable cushioned benches. I reached for his arm again, wanting the sense of security and peace it had given me.

"How do we know we won't be attacked again?" I didn't like the hint of desperation in my voice, but there it was.

"You don't. Look, I can't explain right now, but I'm hoping you'll be safe, at least for a while. I have to tell you this though; it was *you* the leshy was after, Petal."

He looked briefly distressed and ran his fingers through his long hair as he looked me directly in the eye for the first time that morning. It had a quite devastating effect on me.

His words disturbed me as well. I had hoped for reassurance that last night was completely random and that things would go back to normal now. And what on earth was a 'leshy'? He must have meant the bus driver. I opened my mouth to ask, but he stopped me with a finger on my lips. My breath caught at this unexpected and intimate contact.

"Just stay safe, Petal. For me." He reached for my hand suddenly and placed it over my hip pocket. "Keep this on you at all times," he whispered.

Confused, I put my hand in my pocket. The mysterious torch was still there. It was warm and smooth and impossible to avoid stroking. How amazing that it had stuck with me through last night's adventures. I looked up again, full of questions, but Indigo was gone.

I turned to my friends, expecting them to comment on his sudden departure, but they were focussed on the menu. My stomach grumbled loudly, which told me why they were oblivious to my conversation with Indigo. A clock on the wall told me it was nearly lunchtime. I leaned over Cherie's shoulder to look at the menu and she smiled briefly at me, then reached up to touch my hair.

"You've got your fresh flowers back, Jas," she said as if this was perfectly natural, "and they're so pretty."

4 THE MORNING AFTER

The flowers dropped from my head one by one as we ate breakfast. No-one else in the café seemed to notice my disturbing floral problem. It was a noisy place, with a lot of happy chaos. Apart from Josh and Cherie's grumbles about the way Indigo had ignored their questions and disappeared so rudely, we were all quiet as we demolished breakfast. I seldom eat in cafés as my parents don't believe in spending money on eating out. This is a bit hypocritical given that they own a takeaway business.

I couldn't stomach my favourite breakfast of bacon, eggs, and sausages. In fact, just looking at the huge piles of meat on Josh and Tina's plates made me feel sick. Instead, I had mushrooms in a delicious creamy sauce on toast.

Josh eventually put down his knife and fork and cleared his throat to start the conversation no-one wanted to have about last night. He was prevented by Tina and Cherie's phones ringing. When Cherie answered, I could hear her mum chewing her out for staying out all night without permission. I heard Josh and Tina's grandad's concerned voice on a similar topic. Tina apologised and reassured him before hanging up.

Cherie's mum went on and on until we were getting

looks from the tables near us. Cherie hung up in exasperation and looked away, drumming her fingers on the table. Her phone rang again straight away.

"Mum! I know, I'm sorry, alright? Oh … Hi, Mrs Read, yes she's right here. She's totally fine. I'll hand her over." My phone had been in the back pocket of my shorts last night so it must be at the bottom of the ocean now.

"Jasmine." My mother sighed into the phone, and I realised what a complete troll I had been for not calling her as soon as I woke up. "Harry rang us hours ago to tell us about your accident and we've been trying to find you ever since! Where are you? Why did you even go into the city without telling us last night? Are you okay?" I could tell Mum wanted to go on, but she stopped there. She wasn't yelling. She just sounded very worried.

"Mum, I'm so sorry. Look I'm totally fine now, you don't need to worry at all."

"Well, I am worried, Jasmine. How could you fall off a ferry? That's so … ridiculous. Tell me, where you are now, and we'll come get you."

It took me a fair while and a lot of repetition to convince my mother that I was fine and that I could get myself home. My baby brother Harrison started howling (helpfully for once) in the background and I hung up to find my friends watching me.

"Okay," I said. "Let's start with what happened to the bus driver after I fell off the boat."

Cherie and Josh exchanged glances and Tina looked down at her plate. Then Cherie leaned in, talking in a low voice. We had to huddle in to hear her over the café noise.

"Jas, I don't say this to freak you out, babe, but you should be dead right now," she began.

This was not a good start, and I found my body reacting to the memory of the dark water dragging me down. Cherie went on to explain how Indigo had charged out of nowhere seconds after I fell overboard and grabbed the bus driver, throwing himself and the creature over the side.

Cherie and Josh had both been on the receiving end of the bus driver's unnatural strength. They were confounded by how Indigo had managed to wrestle him over the side. But Cherie's explanation grew even weirder. She described how the water had boiled where they went over, and several sea birds dive-bombed the spot where the pair had entered the water.

The birds disappeared, and a mini tornado formed over the water and swept up a heavy-looking object before spiralling up into the sky and out of sight in the dark. All of this happened in the space of a minute and apparently no one else on the ferry saw it. The boat moved away from the action, taking its light with it, so that's all Cherie saw. She and Josh wanted to jump in after me, but Tina convinced them that my best chance lay with turning the boat around. There was no way they could have found me without its light. By the time they had raised the alarm and the boat had turned, a full half hour had passed. It was another half hour before they found Indigo in the water, holding my still body in his arms. My friends were very agitated by then, convinced that I was gone.

"You shouldn't have stopped me jumping in," Josh interrupted. "If Indigo hadn't found her, it would have been too late by then."

Tina looked at Josh with an agonised expression as Cherie continued.

"When they pulled you out of the water, Jas, well, you didn't look good. The truth is you didn't look alive. Then Indigo … um … he bent down and kissed you." Cherie held up her hand at Josh, "No, I know you think it was CPR, but from where I was standing, it was a kiss, plain and simple. Then … well you know the rest."

I closed my eyes and was swamped by intense fear, as if something bad was about to happen. My heart sped up and the shaking I had been able to hide earlier became uncontrollable. *The icy grip of dark water was pulling me down to oblivion.*

"Jas! Jas, are you alright?!"

Cherie had noticed that I was gripping the table tightly, desperate not to make a scene in the café. Then Tina was there, stroking my back and talking quietly to me.

"Jas, it's okay. Nothing bad is happening to you. You're alright. We're right here with you." She kept repeating this sort of thing until the feeling of dread and the shaking stopped. I drew a deep breath and opened my eyes.

"Woah, what was that? I'm sorry, guys, I don't know where that came from. I'm alright now." I wasn't, of course; how could I be?

"I think you had a panic attack. It's not surprising after all you've been through," Tina said.

"Thanks, Tina. How did you get so wise?" I attempted to smile at her, but she looked down and shrugged.

Without touching my head, I could tell there were flowers in my hair again. A close look from Tina confirmed this, but everyone kindly said nothing. Cherie spoke into the silence, looking at me the whole time, wary of my fragile mental state.

She told me that Indigo had convinced them I'd be safer at his place than at the hospital. Tina had been worried about secondary drowning, but I was showing no symptoms and given the way Indigo had dealt with the bus driver, my friends decided to take his advice.

"Also, you've seen the way Indigo sweeps you along and doesn't give you a chance to say no. He even managed to fend off the cops at the dock. We were all exhausted and we didn't know where else to go, so we went with him." Josh took up the story, pronouncing Indigo's name carefully, in the way you do when you don't really like a person but are trying to be fair-minded.

"It was kind of him, when he didn't even know us," Tina said.

Cherie continued. "He was also elusive. Before you ask, Jas, he didn't give us any meaningful answers about anything although he seems to know exactly what's going on."

Cherie hesitated.

"Don't walk on eggshells around her now. She's way stronger than you think, and she needs to know," Tina said.

Cherie bit her lip and looked doubtful, so Tina carried on.

"Indigo believes that it was only you that the bus driver – he called it a leshy – was after, Jas."

"That's really insane. There's nothing special about me."

It hadn't escaped my notice that all this trouble, which had started with Chad and continued with the bus driver, was targeted at me. Indigo and his father had confirmed this when I overheard them this morning, but I decided to keep this to myself for now. The whole conversation had been weird, and I didn't want to worry my friends even more. I suspected they would be better off as far away from me as possible right now.

"It's time we went home, I think. I need to be alone for a while to digest all this."

Cherie snorted. "Yeah right, Jas, like we're going to leave you to deal with all these weirdos by yourself."

Was she including Indigo in that? Possibly. Despite his heroics, I couldn't blame her for thinking he was weird.

"Jas!" Josh spoke loudly. I had drifted off, thinking about Indigo. How ridiculous that my life was in danger, and I was thinking about a boy.

"Earth to Jasmine."

I tried to look more attentive as he carried on.

"No-one is going to let you deal with this by yourself, okay? Before we go, you need to tell us what happened with you and Chad in the grapevines."

"Alright," I said. "Chad hauled me into the vines and attacked me. He tried to kiss me, and he was very persistent and physical … umm, I don't want to talk about that. Anyway, some grapevines grew out of nowhere and wrapped themselves around him, pinning him to the ground like something out of a horror movie."

Josh swore uncharacteristically. "Don't worry, Jasmine,

I'll find that bastard and sort him out."

Cherie also swore and Tina looked angry. They both added similar opinions on Chad and what we should do about him.

"Please don't, guys. I'll talk to the police about Chad. I don't want him to attack anyone else."

Everyone nodded grimly in agreement.

"It's a good start, Jas, but if I ever see that creep…"

I interrupted Cherie. "I have a feeling his attack is related to the bus driver somehow. What *is* going on?" I was trying to move past Chad and his attack. It made me uncomfortable talking about it.

No-one had any answers for me, though, and we agreed to keep the unbelievable parts of the story to ourselves. We scraped our chairs back and headed to the counter to pay for breakfast. None of us had thought that through when Indigo deposited us here. I had no money with me, having left home with just enough cash to get into the Fiesta del Sol, and my public transport card. I'd have to borrow from Tina or Cherie.

"That blonde guy who came in with you already paid for your food, sweeties," said the man behind the counter. He winked at us then went back to frothing milk.

None of us could figure out when Indigo had paid, given the speed he departed. I didn't like that he'd paid for us. I was indebted to him already and determined to get back on an equal footing with him somehow…if I ever saw him again.

"That was super sweet of him," Tina gushed.

I kept my thoughts to myself and agreed it was a nice gesture, but Cherie muttered something about hidden agendas and Josh scowled deeply.

The ferry trip home was rough due to strong winds. The boat shuddered and bumped its way through the short space of open water between the mouth of Auckland Harbour and the calmer waters of the volcanic islands near Waiheke. This sort of ferry motion had never bothered me before, but it did today. Now I couldn't look at the water without feeling a burst of abject terror. As long as I kept the fear compartmentalised and focussed on my friends' faces, it stayed relatively contained. I wondered if I'd always feel this way on the ferry now. If so, I was going to avoid leaving the island for a long time to come.

Sensing my stress, Cherie leaned into me and put her arm around my shoulders. I was further distracted by Tina and Josh. They were locked in a quiet argument, communicating with angry looks and hand gestures. We'd seen them use their own twin language before, though usually it was less heated and never lasted this long.

"What do you think they're arguing about, Jas?" Cherie asked.

They were quite fascinating to watch.

"Probably about whether or not to stay away from me and the scary freak show that's following me around," I muttered darkly.

"It's not all bad though, is it Jas?" Cherie winked at me, and I knew where this was going. "Indigo's a total babe. You really couldn't have asked for a better-looking hero."

I pulled a face. "Cherie, you called him a weirdo with a hidden agenda an hour ago!"

"Yeah … well … just trying to look on the bright side, you know. Sure, he has some annoying qualities, and his personality is pretty much Mr Frosty." Her face brightened again "But there was also Hot Hero Number One … nothing wrong with him!"

"Hot Hero Number One," I groaned. "What *are* you talking about?"

"Oh, *come on,* Jasmine: the guy in the vineyard last night!"

"Ah yes." I couldn't help smiling softly as I remembered. How could he have slipped my mind for even a moment? In fairness, a lot had happened since I met him. "There was nothing wrong with him."

"Why, Jasmine Read, that is the closest you have ever come to admitting you *like* a boy! This is truly a momentous moment," Cherie chirped in a Scarlett O'Hara imitation.

I pictured her in a large flouncy southern belle dress, talking and lazily waving a lacy fan. Distracted by my imaginings, I noticed too late that Cherie had whipped out her phone and taken a photo of me in all my bedraggled glory.

"Cherie! Don't you dare post that. I haven't had a shower for two days and my hair is probably full of weeds." I tried to snatch her phone off her, but she was too quick.

Chortling, Cherie slipped out of reach and jabbed at her phone in a 'send' motion.

I slumped in defeat, imagining the myriad social media accounts she had just posted my wretched appearance on.

"You don't really think I'd do that to you, do you?" said Cherie with a mock hurt look. "I just emailed it to myself to use as ammo later in case I need it." She smiled sweetly, then sighed a bit sadly. "Look, here we are, home again on little old Waiheke."

There was less wind on the island than out on the open water, and it was a lovely warm afternoon when we docked at the wharf. The sight of the sheltered harbour made me sigh with relief. The bush-clad hills embraced us on three sides, and birds were singing in the trees near the terminal. I could see Mum leaning on her car, waiting for me, Harrison on her hip. It all seemed so normal and comforting. A far cry from the events of last night when we had fled from the terrifying bus driver. I was tempted to think that everything would be alright now, but I couldn't believe it after Indigo's warnings.

I glanced over at Tina and Josh who were still glaring at each other. Their expressions and body language mirrored each other perfectly. I managed to catch Josh by himself as Tina and Cherie went down the gangway in front of me.

"Josh, you guys need to stay away from me until I figure this out. I don't want any of you getting caught in the crossfire again." I would have carried on, but Josh stopped me with a look.

"No, Jasmine. We're not going to leave you at the mercy of some weird creatures. Or alone with Indigo for that matter."

"Is that what you guys were arguing about?" I asked him.

"Not really. He did come up, but mostly I was trying to convince Tina to stay at home with Koro until we deal with your problems. I don't think she's up to any more horrifying experiences. I'm going to take her home now, then I'll come over to your house, okay?" Tina and Josh lived with their grandad, as their parents both worked on an oil rig somewhere in the South China Sea.

I agreed with him about Tina, but I didn't want him at risk either. There was no time to say more though, as my mum swooped in and wrapped me in a big hug. I sagged against her and surprised us both by holding onto her tightly for a long time. Tears leaked from my eyes, but I quickly wiped them away before anyone could see.

"Oh Jasmine, I'm so glad the sea didn't keep you, honey." Mum finally stepped back, leaving one arm around my shoulders as she led me away from ferry.

She called out to my friends, thanking them for bringing me back safely. From the back of Mum's ancient Mini, I saw Josh and Tina being greeted by Koro, their grandad, with a brief hug, and Cherie standing alone, her face closed. Her mum hadn't come to get her, and she accepted a ride home with Tina and Josh.

On the short drive home, Mum cast anxious looks at me in the rear-view mirror. Harrison was howling – he hated being restrained in the car – so she couldn't talk to me. I deliberately sat in the back next to Harrison and held his chubby little hand. Usually his fussing made me irritated, but right now it was helping me feel less anxious. It was a normal and familiar sound in a world that had turned strange and dangerous.

5 A SHOCKING REVELATION

I leapt out of the car as soon as we pulled into the white-shell driveway of our old villa, intent on avoiding Mum until I could decide what to tell her. I didn't know what to say that wouldn't either freak her out or see me spending the summer in counselling sessions. Mum was too quick though. She grabbed my arm and looked at me intently before nodding to herself. Then she gave me the time I needed.

"Right, young lady, meet me in the garden in half an hour and you can tell me all about it."

She headed inside with Harrison, who was cooing quietly now he was out of the car. I walked around the outside of the house smiling to myself at the semi-wild garden that rambled down the hill towards the bush at the end of our property. There was a chaotic mixture of lavender, native plants and wildflowers on one side of the garden and a large vegetable patch on the other. An overgrown lawn abundant with clover and yellow buttercups lay between them. My parents loved to garden with wildlife in mind and believed that lawnmowers were a bee's worst enemy. At the end of the garden a path led on down through the trees to a beach.

I threw my soggy boots aside with relief. I doubted I'd

want to wear them again after their role in my near drowning. My bare feet relished the feel of soft grass as I wandered through the garden. Halfway down the slope, I stopped at my favourite sunny spot on a terrace bordered by blooming sunflowers and unhealthy blueberry bushes. Mum claimed the blueberries must have emotional problems but in reality blueberries prefer peat soils and not the dry clay of Waiheke.

As I stretched out in the sunshine with a gentle breeze ruffling my hair, the events of last night felt far away and unreal. I closed my eyes, enjoying the moment and the feeling of home and safety. My body relaxed in places I hadn't known were tense. A quiet thumping noise drew my attention. At first, I thought it was my own heartbeat, until it gradually grew louder and my body thrummed and shuddered to its rhythm. It was probably the neighbours practicing their drums for a full moon party. I let the drumbeat and the warmth of the sun wash my thoughts away.

"Jasmine."

Mum's soft voice roused me from my semi-conscious state – had it been half an hour already? I was more rested and at peace than I could ever remember feeling. I sat up and pulled my legs beneath me. Regardless of the agreement with my friends, I knew I should tell Mum the whole story.

I left out a few things, like how sweet the stranger in the vineyard had been, and how wonderful but annoying Indigo had been. I also didn't see any reason to mention how close I had come to dying in the water. I watched as Mum took it all in. She didn't reach for her phone to call a counsellor, or yell at me for being a liar and ground me. She just nodded along as if she had heard this sort of story before.

"Well then," she sighed. "I suppose this has to do with your biological father."

My *what*? Reality shifted, and I grabbed the nearest sick blueberry bush to anchor myself.

Mum took a deep breath. "You see, I met this amazing guy one Beltane when I was crowned May Queen." Her expression became dreamy. "I was sure it was best to wait till you were older to tell you this, but I guess you are *older* now…" She trailed off, looking past me with a strange expression.

I spun around to see what she was looking at. The blueberry bush I had been grimly clutching was no longer a spindly thing, with a few sad green berries. Now it was a lush two-metre-high bush with fat, ripe berries clustered liberally on its branches.

"This seems to be happening when I get emotional," I offered. "And my hair…"

"My Goddess, your hair," Mum interrupted. "Night-blooming jasmine. And in the daytime too!" She plucked a berry and popped it into her mouth. "Delicious. You try them, sweetie."

"Mum! Why aren't you freaked out by this? Something weird is going on. And what on earth did you mean about my *real* father?" She really didn't seem worried about the bush, or the flowers growing out of my hair. It was as if she had seen it all before.

"Not your real father, Jasmine. Your *biological* father - he had a way with plants too…" She smiled, lost in memory. "Your real father is up at the house fixing you a special birthday – and thank goodness you're still alive – lunch."

I had a moment of guilt. Dad had never given me any reason to think he was not my real father. He had done everything you would expect from a father and more. But they had both lied to me! It was unbelievable. What was Mum thinking, dropping a bombshell like this on me? Especially after the night I'd just had.

"Anyway," Mum continued. "I'm afraid I can't tell you much about your biological father. He was exotic, tall, fabulous company and we had a wonderful couple of weeks together. Oh and he was very spiritual - so in touch with his sacred masculine and feminine sides."

"Couple of weeks!" I grimaced choosing to ignore the spiritual mumbo jumbo and focus on facts. "What was his name?"

Mum frowned, her nose wrinkling, eyes squinting. It was the look she wore when she was stalling for time.

"For heaven's sake, Mum. Don't tell me you can't remember!"

"I can, I can. Just give me a second. It was … very unusual. I have it written down somewhere. I think it was Nyall. Yes, that's it. Nyall. He was American." Then she winced. "I was practicing natural birth control and it's usually so reliable I never thought I would become pregnant. So, I didn't ask for his last name. I met your dad shortly after Nyall left."

I couldn't think of anything to say that didn't include me yelling at Mum and calling her unforgivable names. So, I said nothing, and a gnawing feeling took hold in the pit of my stomach.

"Say something, Jasmine. Yell at me. Call me a stupid old hippie. But don't clam up on me when you're angry. It's not good for your inner balance, sweetie."

I glared at Mum as I stood up and stormed away in a fog of anger. I stormed right into Dad coming down the lawn. He smiled and swept me up in a giant hug.

"Jasmine. You really gave us a scare, sweetie". Dad tucked me under his chin in a way he hadn't done for years, wrapping me in comfort and safety. I couldn't stand it for long though. I opened my mouth to accuse him of lying to me all my life, but his attention had been drawn to the front gate.

I followed his gaze and froze. Chad stood there, staring at us. When he saw us looking, he shrugged and shook his head vigorously, then turned and hobbled down the lane, as if he was in pain.

Spurred by sudden anger, I broke away from Dad and ran after him. I needed to know why he'd attacked me, and what it had to do with all the other events of last night. As

I ran down the driveway with shells cutting into my bare feet, Dad called after me.

"Jasmine. What on earth are you doing?"

I didn't answer. Chad was now running down the middle of the narrow street, with no hint of a limp. There are no footpaths on our street, only wide grass verges, which the islanders prefer. I guess it makes them feel a bit closer to nature. With my bare feet, I stuck to the verge, minding out for muddy spots. Chad was way ahead of me when he turned the corner.

He glanced back and blew me a jaunty kiss that was totally out of place with the angry-crazy look in his eyes. By the time I reached the corner he'd gone, but I nearly crashed into Cherie who was coming from the other direction.

"Woah there, Jas. Who or what are you running from now?" She looked around, then brightened. "Nothing scary. Just your dad."

"I'm not running away!" I wheezed. "I was chasing Chad, but he disappeared. You must have seen him running towards you. Unless he went into someone's backyard."

"I didn't see anyone except you. Are you sure it was Chad? You've been through a lot lately and…"

"Jasmine! What are you doing chasing guys down the road? Where did he go anyway? Oh – hi Cherie." My dad smiled distractedly.

I threw a triumphant look at Cherie as Dad backed up my story.

She shrugged. "Well, let's just add it to the list of crazy stuff."

"Dad, I have to talk to you about something Mum just told me …" I glanced at Cherie, but I knew my good friend could handle it okay. I couldn't let the whole biological father thing go right now, even with all the other weird things going on. Besides, I had a terrible feeling that it was all connected.

"Can it wait till after waffles, pumpkin?" Dad asked.

"No, Dad, it can't. Mum just told me that you aren't my

biological father! Is that true?" A surge of anger rose in me again. It was unbelievable that my parents had kept this hidden for so long. I could understand my mum shoving this sort of thing under the carpet, but Dad? I had never felt so betrayed.

"What? That's ridiculous! Who told you such rubbish?"

His genuine look of surprise made me pause. Was it possible that Dad didn't know this sordid family secret?

Cherie looked at us both and wisely said nothing for once.

"Mum just told me this now in the garden. We think it's related to why I was attacked last night."

"What? Maybe you should tell me the whole story before we go and talk to your mum." Dad looked grim, and I suspected Mum was in for big trouble.

So, right there on the street corner I quickly told him everything that had happened last night. He might as well know since Mum did, though he was far less likely to believe it all. Dad doesn't join in with Mum's maypole and naked midnight dancing – not to my knowledge.

Dad's face grew more incredulous as I went on, even though Cherie chipped in several times with helpful comments like, "It's totally true!" and "Totally!" She accepted it as perfectly natural that I would tell my parents everything, despite our agreement not to tell anyone. When I'd finished, Dad looked at us with an unreadable expression.

"Let's go and talk to your mum about all this, shall we?"

Without waiting, he stalked off towards the house. Cherie and I trailed after him. I told Cherie she should really go home and leave us to our family drama, but she shook her head.

"No can-do, babe. I'm not leaving you alone right now with all these crazy things going on. Besides, this is better than a made for tv emergency room drama."

I fumed at Cherie's insensitivity but didn't try to stop her.

We found Mum and Dad in the dining room, cradling a sleeping Harrison and staring morosely at a spectacular meal laid out on the table. Waffles with chocolate sauce, berry compote and whipped cream. My stomach curdled at the sight.

"I'm sorry, Gerald, but it's true," she was saying. "I should have told you years ago. I don't know why I didn't." She managed to appear genuinely confused. "I had a powerful feeling that I just couldn't tell anyone. Not even you." She looked at Dad beseechingly.

"A powerful feeling!" Dad yelled. He stalked into the living room and stared out the bay windows.

I just couldn't believe that Mum had never told Dad about this. It was outrageous.

"Mum… Dad..." I tried, but they weren't listening.

Mum hoisted herself and Harrison – still asleep unbelievably – out of her chair and went after Dad.

"Best leave them to it for now, Jas," said Cherie.

She was familiar with discord in her house, but it was rare for me. Mum and Dad only bickered occasionally over everyday stuff and seldom yelled at each other and never like this. And it was my fault. Well, Mum had a lot to do with it, but I would never have brought it up like that if I'd known that Dad didn't know. Cherie and I slipped down the hall to my bedroom at the back of the house. Before we could close the door, Dad swooped in dramatically and scooped me up in a suffocating squeeze.

"You are, in every way that counts, my daughter, Jasmine," he proclaimed. "Nothing has changed. Do you hear me?"

He didn't wait for an answer but swept out again. Moments later he and Mum were yelling again, joined by Harrison's distressed cries. I tried to block it out.

"Intense drama, dude" Cherie exclaimed, "really intense. I never would have suspected Gerald wasn't your old man."

I slumped down in the cheerful window seat, lavender waving at me through the open windows.

"Can I just have a moment, Cherie? I mean, can you leave me alone for a while?"

"Sorry, babe but you are stuck with me" she replied cheerfully. "Josh and I are going to hang around until you're out of danger from surfer dudes, monsters, or good-looking Nordic blokes."

"Oh, Jas," she said, her empathy kicking in as flowers rained down around my face. She sat down next to me and put her arm around me. I laid my head on her shoulder as tears welled up and I was glad she hadn't left me alone to wallow in self-pity.

Cherie picked up a flower and idly sniffed it. "This whole biological dad thing has got you really upset, hasn't it? But *nothing* has changed for you – you'll see. Gerald is the best dad ever."

I felt guilty for feeling so sorry for myself. Cherie's dad had left when she was two and I hadn't seen any great replacements from the steady stream of boyfriends her mum had had since then. I knew I still had a right to be upset, but Cherie was right. I had two parents who loved me and for that I could be grateful. I straightened up and brushed the flowers off my lap. Mum chose that moment to pop her head in to talk to me, but I wasn't ready to forgive her yet and closed the door on her. Dad came in with more proclamations of fatherhood and told me not to worry about him and Mum.

"I know, I know!" I told him and he left us again, promising to talk to me soon about last night. I knew he wasn't on the same page as Mum in believing the full story, so I wasn't looking forward to that conversation.

Cherie and I idled away the rest of the afternoon, listening to music, gossiping about nothing and nobody much. Cherie wanted to talk about Indigo and Hot Hero No.1, but I steered her away from this subject. We lay on my bed with the sun caressing our skin and a gentle breeze wafting in through the window. No more flowers grew out of my head, and the plants stayed outside doing their own thing, unbothered by me. It was a return to normality which I fervently hoped would last, but I couldn't help dwelling on the question of who my biological father really was, and what he might have to do with the current mess I was in.

6 PEACE INTERRUPTED

Our peaceful evening was disturbed when the front doorbell rang. It was growing dark, and I was beginning to feel anxious again.

Dad called out to us, "Jas, Cherie – please come and talk to Duncan."

"I can't believe you called the cops, Gerald. They aren't going to be any help." Cherie muttered as we joined Dad and Duncan (Tina and Josh's uncle) in the dining room. Mum was notably absent.

"Hi girls," Duncan greeted us, ignoring Cherie's rudeness as he sat down at the table. He had known all of us since we were babies but was always 'the cops' to Cherie.

I was unsure what to say to Duncan, but he was a good guy, and *I* didn't want to be rude, so I gave him a pared back version of events, minus the supernatural elements and my near drowning. I just told him that a strange guy attacked me on the ferry before he fell overboard. Cherie didn't say a word and nor did Dad. Dad looked relieved, as if he knew I was telling stories all along – even though I'd never done such a thing before.

Duncan sat quietly throughout, taking notes on a tablet. "That sounds really harrowing Jasmine. I'm so sorry this has happened to you. Can you think of any reason why anyone would want to attack you?"

Duncan put down his tablet and waited for me to answer. I couldn't think of any answer to his question that made sense and so I just stared at my lap and hoped he would move on. After a tense few minutes passed Duncan spoke into the silence and asked what critical information I'd left out, because it was clear to him that several things did not add up in my story. For example, had anyone tried to look for my attacker in the harbour?

My mind raced. I hadn't thought about how it would look that we hadn't told anyone on the ferry about the bus driver going overboard. To me it had been a clear-cut case of 'scary monster mercifully taken down by superhero'. Perfectly acceptable according to Hollywood movie ethics, but perhaps not in reality.

"Hang on, Duncan. What Jasmine left out is that she also went over the side and nearly drowned!" Dad exclaimed.

I had left that out the near drowning because it didn't seem relevant to the complaints I was making against my attackers. I also didn't want to dwell on it. I didn't need another panic attack.

Duncan looked at me with fresh concern. "That *is* a more-than critical piece of information, Jasmine. I'll need more detail about that. I'm going to leave you to rest for now, though. I'll check in with Josh and Tina to see if they have anything to add. In the meantime, I have a harbour search to get underway for your ferry attacker and I'll follow up with Chad Browning about the incident at the dance party."

Cherie and I exchanged worried glances at the thought of Josh and Tina being grilled, or of a monster being dredged up from the harbour. This did not go unnoticed by Duncan as he stood up and moved to the door, talking quietly with Dad. I easily overheard him say that we needed to decide whether to press charges against Chad. He warned that it was often extremely difficult to get a conviction in sexual assault cases without witnesses or more evidence than I'd provided. Dad replied that I was clearly traumatised by last night's events and that he didn't want to push me too hard right now. Before I could hear more, Cherie's phone started singing a rude rap song, and she leaped up in response.

"I gotta go, babe. Don't worry, Josh will be here any second to take over from me." She headed for the door, brushing past Dad and Duncan without so much as an 'excuse me'.

"I don't need babysitting," I hissed at her, but she just tossed me a grin and flounced out the door.

*****

After Duncan left, Dad said that we should decide what to do about Chad later. I gave Dad a quick hug - he was right that I just couldn't deal with it right then. I was exhausted from the day's emotional revelations and the previous night's trauma. Dad did want to talk about everything a bit more but I pleaded exhaustion and headed to bed. As promised by Cherie, Josh was already there, having snuck in my window and made himself comfortable.

"Josh, what are you *doing* here? I don't need a babysitter. Does Koro know you're here?"

"Nope, he's got no idea. Tina's covering for me. She'll tell him I'm sick in my room or something." He gave me a grin. "Also, Cherie gave me a heads-up that I'd better steer clear of home for a while so Duncan can't grill me over last night."

"What about Tina? She'll cave under Duncan's questioning."

Josh looked bummed briefly. "Why didn't I think of that? Ah well, it is what it is. Perhaps it's better if Duncan knows what we were really up against last night. I don't want him coming across trouble unprepared."

"Hmm… I just hope he takes Tina seriously in that case."

Josh was close to his uncle, given his parents' long absences, and no doubt wanted to protect him but it seemed unlikely he would believe what really happened last night. Anyway, we couldn't do much about it now. Having Josh there did make me feel better, even as I berated myself for being selfish, putting him in danger from whatever might befall me next.

"Josh, is this like a sleepover or something?"

"Depends on what you want it to be."

I squirmed at Josh's implication. Whatever he was up to, I wasn't in the mood. I kicked him off my bed and onto the window seat and threw him a couple of blankets. He had to curl his long legs up, but I knew from experience it was perfectly comfortable.

"You can sleep here, but you have to go in the morning. I don't need you or Cherie hanging around like a bad smell."

"Look, Jas, we really need to talk about last night. I think you're still in danger."

"Let's talk about it in the morning. Surely the danger is over with that creepy leshy, or whatever it was, at the bottom of the harbour."

I rolled over, putting my back to Josh as the final word. Something was jabbing into my hip. I hadn't wanted to change into pyjamas in front of Josh, so I was still fully dressed in the comfortable yoga pants and flowy shirt that I had put on when I came home.

"Alright, but only because I know you've had a stressful day with your mum and dad and all."

Josh shuffled around noisily as I suppressed a grumpy reply. Cherie had clearly told Josh about our family drama.

I groped in my pocket and pulled out the object that had been with me since the vineyard that I had at first thought was a torch. Indigo had told me to always keep it with me. I contemplated it briefly before putting it back. It was probably best to take his advice, but it did make me ponder the connection between Indigo and the guy who helped me out in the vineyard after Chad attacked me.

My last thoughts before falling asleep were not of my near drowning, the monster, the torch, or even my parent's revelations and arguments. I pushed all these unpleasant things away and, in their place, came Hot Hero No.1 and Indigo, aka Hot Hero No.2 (according to Cherie's labelling system).

*****

A heavy weight landed on my chest, waking me from a deep sleep. The object in my pocket was uncomfortably hot and vibrating. I opened my eyes to find a huge, hairy bear leaning over me and pinning me down with its paw. When the bear's small dark eyes met mine, its mouth curled back in a sneer that revealed its fangs. I screamed.

The bear's roar threatened to shake the walls down and blasted stinky breath in my face. Josh appeared in the doorway. It was full daylight so he must have gotten up earlier and left my room. Mum and Dad were close behind him. Mum screamed when she saw the bear. Dad went very still.

"Don't move, Jasmine," Dad said quietly.

"What do you think I'm doing?" I squeaked.

"While I distract it, you get out of there fast. Jump out the window and we'll shut the door on it."

Dad continued speaking calmly as he moved Josh and Mum aside. The bear swung its head towards them and narrowed its eyes. I looked at the window - it was torn off its hinges and lay broken on the floor, with bits of glass strewn around the window seat.

"Is that the best you can do, Dad? I thought you were supposed to make yourself bigger with a bear and back away singing," I babbled. The bear was still leaning on my chest.

"We're past the point where that would work."

Dad threw a large flat object at the bear and yelled. "Hey, Yogi. Over here, you big, ugly brute!"

Dad's missile was a hideous picture of my great-grandmother that hung in the hall, freaking people out with its old-fashioned creepiness. Mum loved that picture.

It hit the bear's head and had the desired effect of distraction. It also made the bear very angry. It leaped at the door more nimbly than seemed possible for such a bulky beast.

"Run!" Dad yelled and slammed the door shut.

I threw back my bedclothes and leaped off the bed. I landed awkwardly on broken glass, which bit into my palms and knees before I could scrabble up and out the window in one ungainly motion.

I risked a glance back and saw the bear charging at the door, smashing a paw through it. Then it stopped to look my way, as if it had forgotten something. With a loud snort and a growl, it pulled its paw from the door and came after me.

I sprinted down the garden, panic fuelling me. I heard my parents and Josh yelling after me as I tripped and fell, scraping my knee on the rock wall at the bottom of the garden. I scrambled back to my feet and took the track down to the beach. I had no strategy, in fact my mind was a complete blank filled with animal terror as I hurtled down the narrow path, jumping over tree roots and sliding down the steep, muddy sections I usually navigated with care.

Within minutes, I reached the bottom of the track. The beach was as long as a football field and enclosed by steep bush-covered slopes. The tide was high, leaving only a narrow strip of beach.

I had fled without thought to an isolated place with no help in sight and no viable escape routes.

A track at the far end of the beach led up and around the headland to the ferry terminal and the ridge top road, but I wouldn't be able to outrun the bear uphill, nor could I outswim it. After yesterday, swimming was not my preferred choice. With no options left, I grabbed a piece of driftwood and turned to meet the bear. What I saw made me step back in shock.

The clear track I'd come down moments ago was so

overgrown with bushes, trees and vines, I could barely discern the entrance. Halfway up the hill the bushes were shaking furiously as the bear struggled through the vegetation. As much as it scared me, I recognised that I was the likely cause of the instantaneous plant growth – just as I had caused the vines, the blueberry bush, and the flowers in my hair to grow. If I could harness this new ability to make things grow, I might be able to save myself from the bear the same way I'd saved myself from Chad. The bear might prove a trickier customer than a sleazy surfer, but I had to try. I thought hard trying to make something happen, and when it didn't, I desperately started chanting.

"Grow, trees, grow. Grow, trees, grow. Keep the bear away from me!"

Nothing happened, and the bear burst out of the bushes right in front of me, trailing foliage in its wake. It stood for a moment shaking its head and snorting bits of greenery out of its nose.

"Oh help!" I cried out.

As soon as the cry left my lips three things happened simultaneously. The first thing was an almost unbearable heat flaring in my hip pocket where the torch or whatever it was nestled. The second was a small evergreen tree with spiky needles crashing to the ground, narrowly missing the bear as it scooted out of the way. The third, and most outrageous event, was a wolf the size of a small pony barrelling out of the trailhead at the far end of the beach and bounding towards me in a blur of grey and brown. At the last second it swerved and threw itself, growling and snarling, at the bear.

Bears and wolves! In New Zealand! The only native mammal in this country is a bat. There are no wolves in our zoos, let alone roaming the beaches and bush of Waiheke Island.

The wolf and the bear rolled and scrabbled together with a furious crunching of churned-up pebbles. It was hard to tell the animals apart. Above the din, I heard my parents and Josh calling frantically from the top of the track by our house. At least the new jungle would keep them from the dangers on the beach. Only a gun would stop these animals, and we knew no one on Waiheke with a gun, not even Duncan.

I had to move. I ran for the track the wolf had come out of. My breath came fast, and my feet stumbled over the pebbles. My vision was blurred by sweat and tears when I finally reached the track and I knew the chances of outrunning the winner of the fight behind me were slim.

Speeding around the first corner of the bush track with no caution, I crashed into a hefty guy coming equally as fast the other way. We both went flying to the ground, limbs tangled. My forehead connected with his chin painfully and he let out an involuntary grunt.

I yelled at the poor guy as I tried to untangle myself. "Run! Wolf! Bear!" I sounded crazy, but I didn't care.

The person I had crashed into stopped me from fleeing again with a hand on my arm.

"It'll be alright, there's nothing to fear now" he said, and despite my panic I found myself relaxing a bit even as I pulled back into a crouch ready to take flight again if I needed to. The sound of the animals fighting had gone and in its place was silence.

That meant that one of the beasts was probably stalking us right now. I panicked again and leaped up sobbing, "…the wolf, the bear….!"

As I stood up, I focussed on the guy in front of me finally as he rose too. It was Hot Hero No. 1 and there I was, red-faced and hysterical, sobbing in front of him. He didn't seem concerned by my hysteria, but I was mortified to be seen in such a state by him. I managed to stop crying but I was on the edge and he knew it. He looked me over warily.

I was about to turn and run when we heard rocks being disturbed on the beach - something was coming. Before I could do anything, the wolf appeared around the corner from the beach and leaped onto us pushing us both back down to the ground in a heap. I felt its hot and eager breath on my face and screamed, sure that I was done for this time.

7 HOW TOMAKE FRIENDS WITH WOLVES

"Jasmine, it's okay," said Hot Hero No 1. "Churros is my friend."

Laughing, he pushed the wolf off us and sat up. The wolf carried on leaping all over him like a puppy. He gave up and threw his arms around the wolf.

"Are you hurt, Churros?" He looked intently into the wolf's eyes. "Where did the bear go?"

I was jealous of the wolf receiving this attention from … well, I needed a name. I couldn't carry on calling him Hot Hero No. 1, even if he and his wolf had just saved me from the bear.

The wolf and his boy communed, gazing into each other's eyes and completely ignoring me.

"Don't you think we should get out of here? I don't know where the bear's gone, but it might be back any second."

I didn't want to interrupt them, but I was still worried about the bear.

The wolf turned and captured my gaze. A distant howl sounded in the back of my mind, and I felt the same sense of reassurance that I had from the eagle in the bedroom. I didn't question this interaction; my worldview had shifted over the past couple of days to the point where I accepted this as the new normal.

"Come on then," the wolf's companion said. "Let's get you somewhere safe."

"But what about the bear?" I repeated. "Is it gone?"

The giant wolf tilted its head at me and gave a few soft yips.

"Churros says it's fine, Jasmine. The bear has fled for now. Churros is stronger in spirit, so it won't attack you again while he's here."

"How come you and your giant pet wolf came rushing to my rescue just then? Was it coincidence that you were at the dance party the other night as well?"

"My apologies, Jasmine. You're right. Circumstances have prevented me from being courteous. I am Carlos Enrique Camero, and this is my companion, Churros. The island told me you were in danger and led me here."

I really needed more information about the strange and deadly things happening to me. But this guy - Carlos - was as vague and cryptic with his answers as Indigo was. I reflected on how Carlos had given me the object that Indigo had subsequently told me to keep safe. The same one still in my pocket now. Whatever was going on, these two strange guys were clearly connected and at the heart of my troubles.

"There is more to tell you, Jasmine, but now is not the time."

He stood up and held out his hand to help me up. He didn't look much older than me, but I felt safe with him. As safe as I had felt with Indigo. Also, I did agree with him that lingering near where the bear had last been seen was not ideal, so I stored my questions away and let him pull me up and lead me up the path away from the beach. Carlos and Churros moved silently and swiftly up the steep slope, as if they were on the flat. Carlos didn't look back and I felt a moment of loss out of the bright light of his attention. I hated it when someone made me feel that I needed to be noticed by them all the time. Either they were my best friend forever or they were out of my life permanently. Nothing in-between would do.

I trudged behind them, soon out of breath and preoccupied. If I went home before my 'problems' were resolved, I would put my family and friends in danger, and sooner or later there would be collateral damage. On the other hand, Mum had answers that I needed. I was sure she hadn't told me everything about my biological father and Dad would be desperate if he couldn't protect me. Also, I had nowhere else to go. I had a bit of money saved up from working at the fish and chip shop, but I was under no illusion about how long it would last.

By the time we reached the quiet lane running along the top of the hill I was limping from pain in one knee, out of breath from our fast pace and cradling my still-bleeding hand. Realising I'd just suffered another attack on my life, I was suddenly overwhelmed with fear again. My scalp itched as jasmine grew out of my head. It shed stems and flowers when they grew too large and littered the path behind me.

My hands were shaking, and my breath quickened. I tried to focus on the spectacular bush-covered slopes and glistening ocean laid out before me, but it wasn't helping.

"I just need to stop for a second." I lowered myself down to the road verge and sat down hugging my knees to me.

Carlos looked at me for the first time since we'd started up the hill. I closed my eyes, trying to get a grip before panic overtook me – not now in front of Carlos!

"Jasmine, we should keep moving. Although the bear will not attack you again right now, I would prefer it if you were not out in the open in view of prying eyes."

He glanced around as if expecting someone to be staring at us. He came closer and his expression grew concerned.

I basked in his full attention again. Dammit, I had only just met him and it already felt like I'd miss him when he left.

"Jasmine, you are bleeding. Why didn't you say something? And ... you are not coping well, are you?" He reached for my hand.

I pulled it away gruffly. If I pushed him and his kindness away now, I could keep my self-respect and cope when he disappeared back to whatever exotic location he had come from.

"I'm fine." It was getting harder to breathe, though, and my heart palpitated as a now familiar black wave of fear started to overcome me. *The icy grip of cold dark waters was pulling me down to oblivion.*

"You're not fine."

I was caught in my own private nightmare as he gently hauled me to my feet.

"I will need to carry you Jasmine" he said and looked at me for permission. I nodded feebly and he whisked me off my feet and cradled me in his arms. He strode off down the road as if I were no weight at all. His hand stroked my arm and the panic melted as if by magic. A sense of wellbeing and peace came over me, not unlike the one I'd found in the garden the day before. I accepted this gratefully, even though it defied logic. It had taken a lot of time and effort from Tina to sort me out when this had last happened.

No longer taken by panic, I noticed the warmth of his skin close to mine and his strong earthy scent. His nearness sent thrills through my body, and I trembled slightly. I tried to hold myself away. Carlos looked straight ahead, carrying me as if I were a sack of potatoes. Churros ambled alongside, occasionally licking my good hand. Oddly enough, it was comforting.

We turned into a discreet gravel driveway that curved gently away from the road. Sun filtered through overhanging trees and dappled our clothes with green. The driveway led to a small wooden villa in a bright clearing, a charming garden filled with flowers and herbs, overgrown and a bit wild. It was a typical Waiheke Island scene, comforting in its familiarity.

"You live here? I've never seen you around before."

Carlos looked at me for the first time since he had hauled me into his arms. His face was red as if he was blushing, though it was probably just from exertion.

"It's a holiday rental. My parents set me up here for the summer."

He pushed open the unlocked door (what did he and his wolf have to fear, after all?) and stepped into a small kitchen. It was beautifully renovated, cosy and super-tidy. The kitchen merged into the living room. White predominated a vaguely nautical theme not uncommon in Waiheke homes. It complemented the ocean view from the bay windows in the living room – similar in orientation and vibe to our own living room. This guy's parents must be wealthy to rent their son a place for the summer on Waiheke like this - and trusting. Most guys his age would be having a non-stop party by now.

Carlos went to put me down on a sofa covered with a white linen spread.

I let out a small shriek. "Not there! I'll get blood on the sofa."

He made an exasperated sound and placed me gently on a wooden chair at the kitchen table then disappeared down a hallway off the living area. I let out a sigh, loss and relief warring in me as Carlos moved away.

I had to get away from Carlos if I didn't want to fall for him. He was clearly just passing through and no doubt had some stunning Latin girl waiting for him wherever he came from. I imagined a female version of Carlos, she rushed into his arms and laid her head on his shirtless chest...

I was snapped out of my imaginings when Carlos returned. With his shirt on. I had to get a grip. He looked at me oddly and I was worried my thoughts were plastered all over my face. Cherie often tells me I'm an open book.

"Give me your hand," he instructed. He had a first aid

kit, so I mutely uncurled my hand onto the table. It was a complete mess and I found it hard to look at, even though I'm not squeamish.

Carlos pursed his lips. "Churros" he called, and the wolf leaped up from under the kitchen table.

Churros put his paw on my knee and looked up as if asking my permission. I didn't know what for but nodded anyway. He sat up on his haunches, front paws on the table and bent his head to gently lick my injured hand.

"Argh!" I tried to pull away, partly because it hurt and partly because it was gross being slobbered on.

Carlos gripped my arm and looked into my eyes. "Trust me, Jasmine. I know this is strange for you with your trust in medicine and cleanliness. Churros will help heal your hand and dull the pain."

With Carlos looking at me like that, I was helpless to resist, despite how kooky it seemed. The pain had already reduced. I snuck a quick look at my hand and saw that the blood and dirt were gone. A nasty gash ran across the palm. Churros gave one final lick and pushed back from the table. He looked at my knee and started in on that, too. Blood was oozing from a giant rip in my jeans. I absently stroked Churros on the head with my uninjured hand, luxuriating in his soft fur. Carlos gave me a strange look as I did so and reached up as if to touch his own head before he stopped himself.

"This will need stitches, Jasmine, and I don't want you going anywhere now, so we cannot seek out a doctor. Do you trust me? You will feel no pain, thanks to Churros." He looked at me again and I could only nod. By now, I trusted him completely. Not for the first time I wondered how he could be so serious and self-possessed when he was clearly not much older than me.

He also looked like he really knew what he was doing as he deftly sterilised some equipment, took thread from his first aid kit and sewed my hand up. Then he turned his attention to my knee which was bruised and slightly swollen and placed a bag of ice on it. When he'd finished fixing me up, he reached into his pocket and pulled out a phone.

"Call your family, amiga, but don't tell them where you are. Others might be listening, and you do not want to endanger your loved ones by drawing them into your situation right now."

I gasped. How selfish I'd been, not to do this earlier. Josh and my parents must be frantic. But what was I going to say? That some random stranger who knew my name, looked like a male model, and had a spirit animal, had rescued me from the bear with his wolf. Better just to text them.

- Bear gone, I'm safe. Will call soon. Love Jas -

"Better turn that phone off now, or it's going to ring until you answer it," I told Carlos as he gave me scissors to cut the leg of my critically damaged yoga pants. I sighed at the loss of my comfy pants but figured I could turn them into shorts later. Once he had finished, Carlos wrapped my knee in a bandage and then smiled. "It's fine. My number will not show up. Don't you think you should call them though, not just text?"

"No, I don't actually." Besides not knowing how to explain Carlos, I didn't want Mum getting hysterical on the other end of the phone. I was still angry with her, too, and a mean part of me relished how worried she'd be right now.

Carlos narrowed his eyes but said no more.

I changed the subject. "Where are you from anyway? You sound like you're from South America or the US."

"I'm from the US, but I grew up both there and in my family home in Peru."

I'd never met anyone from Peru. Plenty of Americans, of course, who joined the influx of tourists in summer to Waiheke Island. Carlos was an interesting mix of exotic heritage, just like Indigo. And Churros reminded me of the giant eagle in Indigo's bedroom in the city. The dots were connecting. Both had told me the object I still carried in my pocket was important as well.

"You don't know Indigo, do you? A Scandinavian guy who does a mean line in mysterious, just like you?"

He sighed at my question and looked out the window, eyes on the waters sparkling in the distance. Finally, he looked back at me. I squirmed under his serious gaze.

"In truth, Jasmine, I do not know how much to tell you. Anything I tell you may have unintended consequences. Perhaps you could tell me what happened to you after the vineyard, and then I will tell you everything I safely can. What happened between you and Indigo?"

He asked the question as if it was an afterthought and he didn't really care. Clearly, he knew Indigo though. He spoke his name carefully and with a vague hint of contempt, the way Josh had.

So, for perhaps the fourth time, I told the story of the attack on the ferry, and of how Indigo had rescued me. I left nothing out. I suspected Carlos would find none of it hard to believe and could probably help me understand it.

When I told him about the conversation between Indigo and his father, he stopped me. "Are you sure those were his exact words; the Wind's Kiss?" He sounded shocked, as if I had told him the Queen was having an affair.

"Yes, I'm sure. It sounds weird, right? Do you know what he was talking about?"

"You must have crossed over into Supay's land, and the Wind's Kiss brought you back." Seeing my confusion, he elaborated. "You died, Jasmine, and Indigo brought you back from the dead. There is a price to pay for such things and I don't think you will like it."

Carlos stood abruptly and paced the room several times before striding through the door to the garden. He turned on the threshold, his wolf at his heels.

"Excuse me, Jasmine. This changes things. I have to think."

The door closed firmly behind him. I was left alone to process the bombshell he'd just dropped on me. I had been brought back by a kiss – back from the dead.

8 MAGIC

Carlos was the second person to tell me that Indigo had saved my life with a kiss. I searched my memories, determined to remember what had happened that night on the ferry. Despite the risk of another panic attack, I had to remember for myself what had happened. I stood up and wandered over to the sofa. I sank into its plush surface and closed my eyes, letting all the memories I had locked deep inside slowly resurface.

Indigo had dragged me up from the depths and I had struggled for breath even out of the water. I had lost consciousness and darkness claimed me again. This time it was a soft and welcoming darkness, and I went into it gladly, feeling only relief at the release from pain and fear. Then Indigo had called to me soundlessly. I had felt his lips on mine and his breath in my body, summoning me back from the darkness and into the chaos of life again. That may sound crazy, but it's the best way I can describe it.

The next time I saw Indigo, he'd give me answers, surely. I wouldn't let him use his buttery touch to distract me. If I saw him again. This thought was concerning. Aargh. It wasn't just one strange, gorgeous boy I was falling for, but two. I didn't even know them. It must be the hero effect,

I decided, given they had each rescued me from a bad end. I resolved to put these new and unwelcome feelings away and squash any future developments.

Carlos came back inside as I was reeling from my thoughts. He sat down on the sofa next to the window seat and Churros lay down next to him half on my feet and half on Carlos'. All trace of Carlos' earlier agitation was gone. He sat in silence for a few minutes, his hand resting on Churros' fluffy head, stroking it absently. How wonderful to have such a companion in your life, giving you unconditional love and loyalty. Churros looked up as if he could hear my thoughts and shuffled closer, leaning his long body against my leg. The warm, soft weight of him was soothing.

"You have had a rough time of it, amiga, and I understand why you were suffering such mental pain earlier. But I'm afraid you are still in danger. I won't let you carry on in complete ignorance of what is threatening you any longer, whatever the rules say."

Indigo and his father had also spoken of rules, but rules for what – a game?

"A lot of what I am about to tell you, you may find hard to believe, even with your recent experiences." He looked to see if I was receptive, and I nodded for him to continue. I didn't think much was out of the realm of possibility anymore. My mind was wide open, thanks to flowers growing out of my head, a dog with healing powers, monsters and bears attacking me and, of course, the little incident where I had apparently been brought back from the dead by a kiss.

Carlos began with the bus driver. He agreed with Indigo that the bus driver was not human but rather a spirit of the forest: a leshy. He explained that these creatures were neither good or evil, although in Russian and Slavic folklore they sometimes abducted children. Carlos had never heard of a case of this, though like all myths, he said, there was likely to be a grain of truth in it.

When I asked Carlos why a leshy would possibly want to attack me he looked sad.

"I think an unscrupulous Earth Guardian has forced a leshy to do their bidding. An Air Guardian cannot control a forest creature."

"Wait – a what? What's a Guardian?" None of his explanation was making much sense and this seemed like a material point.

Carlos frowned. "But of course, I am getting ahead of myself. You will not know what a Guardian is."

"I am an Earth Guardian," he said, giving weight to the word Guardian as if I should recognise and respect it, though it just made me think of B-Grade sci-fi movies.

"Guardians are directly descended from the Earth Mother and the Sky Father, the creator couple of the world. Such deities are known to many cultures in various forms and by many names. For example, the Earth Mother is known as Pachamama in South America or Mat Zemlya in Russia - here there is Papatūānuku and Ranginui."

He had a bit of a lecturing tone now, which was not unpleasant to listen to. Clearly, he liked to share his knowledge, unlike Indigo and his father. Mum would love all this stuff. Churros sat still the whole while, letting me stroke his head, grounding me in the here and now as Carlos continued his storytelling.

"Wouldn't that make Guardians gods too then? No, wait. Don't answer that. This is all very interesting, but what does it have to do with my problems?" My voice came out whinier than I meant it to, but Carlos answered patiently.

"No, we are not deities, but nor are we entirely human either. We have abilities that come from the elements of earth and air. From the Sky Father and the Earth Mother. These abilities set us apart, even as we bleed and die as normal humans do."

He leaned across the sofa and captured my uninjured hand gently in his. His scent and nearness overwhelmed me, and I tried to shuffle discreetly away from him. Carlos didn't seem to notice and carried on speaking with his eyes locked on mine.

"Have you not felt a closeness with the Earth recently, Jasmine? Have you not heard her heartbeat awaken you to wonders? Has she not opened herself up to you and responded to your requests for help and to your emotions?"

I squirmed and looked away. It was true that something had happened to me in the garden yesterday. I had such a wonderful rest there and woke to the memory of drumbeats pulsing through my head and body. I had felt a connection to something bigger than myself and it had been wonderful. Then there were the grapevines, the blueberries, the jasmine …

"Yes," I acknowledged. "Something like that has been happening to me."

Carlos nodded as if I had confirmed what he already knew.

"But what does that mean? Are you telling me I'm a … a what did you call it … a Guardian?" If so, I certainly had to talk to Mum about my biological father; he must be the reason for this. Maybe he was a Guardian.

Before Carlos could respond, I heard a voice whisper in my mind: - Petal, I'm coming -

I startled and nearly leaped off the sofa as I looked around and saw no one besides Carlos and Churros. The voice came with impressions of sunshine and an ocean breeze, and I knew that it was Indigo speaking to me even though I couldn't see him.

"What is it, Jasmine?"

"Indigo is here," I replied.

Three seconds later a knock sounded at the kitchen door, sharp and demanding. Indigo didn't wait for an answer, but came in. If Carlos had hackles, they would have risen. Churros' hackles did rise. Indigo looked haggard and worn out, but this did not detract from his physical attractiveness. He wore dark blue jeans and a white linen shirt unbuttoned at the top over a v-neck tee – like the one

I had woken up wearing at his place.

I leaped up, pulling my hand from Carlos', as if I'd been caught in a forbidden act.

"Indigo," I breathed.

"Air Guardian!" Carlos exclaimed. "What are you doing here? The rules forbid you intruding on my habitat."

A harsh shriek pierced the sky and the eagle swooped in through the door and landed on Indigo's shoulder. Indigo staggered slightly as he adjusted to its weight. He looked at Carlos with his trademark smirk. His bird stared at Churros and ruffled its feathers before looking me in the eye. A piercing cry sounded in my head, the cry of a bird of prey in flight.

Great. A bird, and a boy, were in my head. Either that or I was going nuts. I wasn't sure which I preferred.

"I think you would agree that the rules have changed, Kúkalabbi."

I didn't know what Nordic language Indigo was using, but I knew an insult when I heard one.

"Besides, you speak of rule-breaking when here you are telling the girl things you shouldn't."

I stiffened at being called 'the girl'. It was so at odds with the intimate greeting Indigo had just given me in my mind. Carlos did not deny the accusation, though how Indigo had guessed that Carlos was spilling the beans, I could only guess.

"You must agree that she needs to know everything now. Her life is in danger, and she has suffered enough fear already, with no idea of why she is being targeted by forces beyond her experience. You cannot talk about breaking the rules – you gave her the Wind's Kiss! I know enough about your people to know what that means and the advantage it gives you. I can see that there have already been consequences!"

He looked at me when he said the last bit and I suspected he knew about Indigo being inside my head.

"Would you rather she had died?" Indigo retorted. "She

would have if I hadn't given her the Kiss. It's stupid to argue about this. Everything would be lost for your people and mine if we had lost her."

Indigo the icy, Indigo the cool, was very angry now. Somehow, I could read his emotions as easily as my own. For all his apparent coolness he was a hot mess of emotions inside. His anger was largely reflected anger, rather than true anger at Carlos. He was still angry from the conversation with his father earlier. Regardless of the source there was so much testosterone in the air, I was afraid things might get violent.

"Stop it, both of you! And stop talking about me as if I'm not here. I want answers and I want them now. I don't care about your 'rules'. Indigo, I've been attacked again and I'm really worried."

Indigo didn't look surprised, but his stance softened, and he looked directly at me for the first time since his arrival. He stepped closer and put his hand on my arm.

"I know, Petal, I felt your fear and came as fast as I could. But I was delayed by trouble of my own."

"It does not matter. I was here," said Carlos.

"What trouble?" I asked.

Indigo hesitated. Then he shrugged. "We were attacked by several thunder spirits this morning. My father was injured badly. He'll be alright, but it took all our strength to fight them off and to heal him."

Carlos looked grim. "Trouble indeed if the thunder spirits were turned against you. That would mean you have a traitor amongst the Air Guardians. What on earth is your father doing here anyway?" I added thunder spirits to the list of crazy creatures I was mentally creating.

Carlos continued: "We'd best put our differences aside for the moment while we consider this threat."

"And you'll tell me what's going on, too. Everything!" I demanded.

I didn't want the sudden shift in mood to deflect them from the explanations I needed. Indigo's news had given me a new sense of panic. Indigo had dealt so easily with the leshy. What could threaten him? What had I become involved in? Indigo looked at me and laid his hand on my arm again. My agitation receded as a new suspicion grew. It wasn't natural that Carlos and Indigo could affect my emotions with a touch.

"We will tell you what we can," said Carlos.

"You're right, Petal. You do need to know what is happening." It wasn't lost on me that neither of them agreed to tell me *everything*.

There was some fluffing around as Carlos insisted on hot drinks and food for me and we all settled around the kitchen table. He thought I was flagging, I guess, but I suspected he was also being sympathetic to Indigo who eagerly accepted a cup of tea and giant slab of something yellow and dense, which Carlos called corn bread. It was delicious, and I devoured two or three large pieces while Carlos talked. Indigo and Carlos sat as far apart as possible, and both carefully avoided getting too close to me as well. This didn't stop Churros from snuggling up to my legs or Indigo's bird from perching on the chair back behind me and nuzzling my ear softly once or twice with his beak. When Carlos noticed this, he gruffly called Churros over to him, and I missed the warm presence beside me. Indigo narrowed his eyes at his bird but did nothing to call it away.

"I was giving Jasmine a brief history of the Guardians. It is urgent that we discuss the recent attacks, but I don't think we can do that meaningfully until Jasmine understands what we are talking about."

Indigo gave a stiff nod and gestured for Carlos to go on.

Carlos turned to me ready to take up his lecture at the point where he had been interrupted by Indigo's arrival.

"Wait," I said. "Are you going to answer my question? Am I a Guardian?"

"We'll get to that, Jasmine, I promise." Carlos took a long sip of tea before beginning again; he had been talking a lot. He told me how the Guardians were once a united people with everyone capable of using the energy or the lifeforce of earth and air, albeit to varying degrees and strengths. Some Guardians were more closely aligned with the Earth Mother, some with the Sky Father, but all lived and worked peacefully together. This all changed about one thousand years ago when the Guardians more aligned with the Sky Father undertook an unspeakably evil act that split the Earth and Sky Guardians into two separate clans.

Carlos concluded on a sad note. "We are now bitter enemies."

Indigo interrupted: "From our perspective, it was your clan that committed the 'unspeakably evil act', but whatever."

He and Carlos glared at each other.

I cleared my throat. "Okay, whatever problem your people had with each other an *unspeakably* long time ago, surely we can move past that now, unless it's relevant to our current situation."

"Well, it is, and it isn't," continued Carlos. "You see, the Air Guardians stole something very precious to the Earth Guardians and the Earth Mother has been growing more distant to us ever since, because of it."

"Ridiculous," snorted Indigo. "It was your clan that stole something from us! And so the wind has become quieter within us since then." Indigo waved his arms in agitation and knocked over the pot of tea. Tea splashed onto my knee. I leaped up and away from the table. Indigo rushed to my side, exclaiming his apologies, while his bird flapped its wings and created quite a wind in the small space. I waved Indigo off. The tea was already cool.

We all sat back down again, and the glaring went on. This was sounding like one of those clichéd misunderstandings that has caused wars and grief between peoples since time immemorial. I could imagine Cherie if she were here with me. She'd be doubled over with laughter and shrieking, "Can you believe these guys, Jas!"

"Guys!" I pleaded. "Let's just move on before some

weird creatures attack us again."

Carlos hurried on as if this was a distinct possibility.

"Whatever happened to cause our enmity, it has diminished the Earth Guardians' strength – and yes, alright, the Air Guardians' too." He held up his hand to stop Indigo interrupting again.

"Every generation is weaker than the one before and now the situation is dire. Some amongst us feel very little kinship with Pachamama. They have left our clan and live amongst humans, deaf to her heartbeat and spirit. I don't know if that is the same for you, Indigo, amongst your people?"

Indigo only glared.

Carlos carried on regardless.

"This is a big problem for all Guardians. So big that the councils of both clans recently met together for the first time in millennia to discuss it. I was not there, but I heard that the meeting was not productive despite many hours of argument. Everybody finally agreed, however, that the problems we are experiencing are not only linked to the crime of the Air Guardians but also to the burden humanity has imposed on Pachamama. Pollution, climate change, habitat destruction, agrichemicals and so on. The earth, and the atmosphere, are hurting badly, and we can all feel it. Pachamama and the Sky Father are drawing away from both humans and Guardians, taking their blessings and life force with them." Carlos stopped for a moment, looking deeply upset.

I lowered my head, a guilty member of humanity. I was aware of all these problems of course, and I even spent a fair bit of time worrying about them and volunteering with my local stream care group, but none of this seemed to improve matters. It was hard to find time in my daily life to do anything truly meaningful about it. Churros looked up at me and whimpered mournfully.

Indigo sat with his arms crossed and a grim look on his face as Carlos carried on describing how the clans disagreed over what to do about the problems facing humanity and the Guardians.

The Earth Guardians argued that it would be best to reveal themselves and work directly with humans to heal the planet and stop the pollution and destruction. Indigo's people, the Air Guardians, wanted to destroy humanity to protect the planet. As Carlos revealed this shocking claim, Indigo looked intently down at his empty teacup. Wow. I fancied a bloke from a cult of magical, genocidal megalomaniacs. Drat. That was that then, even if there was a remote possibility that he was interested in me. Even if he had saved my life.

"Overpopulation *is* the root cause of most environmental problems," Indigo noted stiffly.

"Well, regardless. The Earth Guardians cannot condone this path. Humanity is a part of the Earth Mother herself and destruction wrought upon them is destruction further wrought upon her. It is also the morally incorrect solution."

It looked like the two of them were doomed to repeat the stalemate of their council meeting. I sighed and steered them back to the material matters at hand.

"Okay, genocide is wrong no matter the reason, but let's park that for now. What does any of this have to do with the danger I'm in?"

"I will get to it Jasmine. But first, as I said, the clan council members could not come to an agreement. That is when our prophets stepped in."

Of course, they would have prophets. What's a good mythological cult without a prophet or two.

"The prophets of both our clans agreed with each other. For the first time in living memory, they both had the same vision from Pachamama and the Sky Father," Carlos paused.

"What did they say?" I spurred him on.

"They said, Jasmine, that *you* can help both our peoples and the Earth Mother herself." Indigo answered my question and used my real name for the first time. Even so,

I couldn't take him seriously and burst out laughing. It was all getting too much. Indigo and Carlos weren't laughing though, as Carlos spoke again.

"Jasmine, you are a descendant of the Guardians, one that none of us knew existed until our prophets spoke, and it is you who will save us all by choosing between Indigo and me – between the Sky and the Earth Guardians. You need to choose which one of us should be granted the power to restore the Earth."

"So, you're both here to convince me to support your cause? Huh." I wasn't surprised they were both trying to charm me now. It was an easy choice then; I would choose Carlos and his peaceful cult, thanks. Not the genocidal Air Guardians. Something wasn't adding up though, and the way Indigo and Carlos were studiously looking anywhere except at me, or each other, suggested a missing piece. I looked at Carlos quizzically.

He sighed. "Well, there is a bit more to it. You must fall in love with one of us, truly and deeply, because only then will you be able to communicate your choice directly to the Earth Mother and Sky Father. Love is the only language a mortal can use that is powerful enough to reach them." Carlos sat back and reached for Churros, looking unsure of himself for the first time since I had met him. He had gone bright red and looked super embarrassed.

Indigo looked at Carlos with disdain. "You didn't need to tell her that part. What will she think of us now!"

He turned to me then and spoke earnestly; an odd look for him, which might have been endearing under other circumstances.

"Neither of us were supposed to tell you any of this, Petal. It's against the rules because it's likely to influence your emotions and choices. But nobody was supposed to be attacking you or us either. I find that there is always something left out of the prophecies. Important details usually." His tone was bitter, but I wasn't trying to figure him out right now. I was angry.

Both looked at me expectantly, but I sat in silence. This was just a big game to them! I was the patsy they were supposed to woo so she'd choose their side in this ridiculous feud. I leaped out of my chair and headed for the door with the intention of getting the hell out of there and away from the only boys who had ever made me *feel* so much! Two boys who were the biggest frauds I had ever met.

9 I (MOSTLY) SAVE MYSELF FOR A CHANGE

I stepped out into a gorgeous summer day and my feet met … nothing. Air swept under me with a whistle and tore me violently off my feet. Before I could cry out, I was swept up into the cloudless blue sky. Wind spun me around furiously till waves of nausea rose in me. I was inside a mini tornado that stole my breath and pummelled me painfully, tearing at my clothes. I could barely see past my hair which had torn loose from its ties and was lashing my face.

Over the noise of the wind, I could faintly hear Carlos and Indigo calling out to me to wait and hear them out. Within moments they arrived outside and saw me twisting through the air. Immediately, Indigo took to the air in a mini tornado of his own, although he wasn't spinning around in his tornado the way I was - more riding in the middle of it where it appeared to be calm. His bird winged swiftly up too. If I had doubted any part of Indigo and Carlos's fantastical story of the Guardians and their powers, I certainly didn't now.

I had too big a lead on Indigo and his bird though, and they weren't catching up. My spinning ascent suddenly halted. Something pulled tight around my waist, cutting painfully into my stomach. A thick green vine had encircled and tethered me to the roof of the house below.

The vine strained at my waist and tugged me downwards while the wind yanked me the other way, until I thought I'd be torn in half. I screamed in pain, but just before it became unbearable, the vine snapped and released me. I shot up, ever higher into the air. Carlos couldn't save me now. I was also soaring away from Indigo so fast that I doubted he could catch me even though his arms were stretched towards me. There was a strain on his face that told me he was trying hard.

Moments ago, I'd wanted nothing to do with Indigo and Carlos, but now I was sick with fear that neither of them could rescue me.

- Petal, I can't reach you. You are one of us. Find the wind in your soul and use it -

The strangeness of Indigo's voice in my head was shocking even in my present predicament but I couldn't deny the sense of genuine anxiety coming from Indigo. He couldn't hide how he felt when he was in my head. I guessed that if he lost me, he lost any chance of winning the power to commit genocide on humanity. His suggestion was a bit far-fetched, though. Sure, I had been doing strange things with plants lately, but that must mean I was, if anything, an Earth Guardian. I couldn't control the wind as well.

Carlos' house, with its green corrugated iron roof was now only one of many, a long way beneath me. As I spun, I caught glimpses of the island stretching below me – a patchwork of green bush and wooden houses bordered by beaches of golden sand or pebbles. The ocean sparkled brightly in the sunshine, dotted with boats of all shapes and sizes.

I should have been afraid. But instead, I was angry. This was not okay. Whoever was doing this had to stop.

"Leave me ALONE!" I shrieked at the wind and shoved

my anger in the direction I was heading, along a trail of funnelling wind that was visible when I looked hard enough.

There was an implosion in the air around me and I was pummelled from all directions by invisible hands. The tornado collapsed and for the briefest of moments, I hung suspended in the air before I started to plummet. The anger that had sustained me left, and I screamed in terror.

Indigo caught me mid-air in a superhuman feat. Beads of sweat broke out on his face and his muscles trembled as he plucked me from the sky and floated us both toward the ground on a cushion of air. He threw a look of triumph at Carlos standing below. Carlos' hands were clenched into fists and he wore an unreadable expression.

As my feet touched the ground and my vision dimmed, I sagged against Indigo. Before I could dwell on how I had been rescued *again,* blackness swallowed me up and I passed out.

*****

I awoke on Carlos' couch with a massive headache and feeling very bruised around my middle. Groaning quietly, I lay still and waited for the pain in my head to pass. My vision was blurry and I was feeling generally worn and battered by all the action I had seen the last few days.

Carlos and Indigo were arguing quietly nearby. As my vision slowly cleared, I saw the two guys at the kitchen table glaring at each other.

"We need to stop the challenge now!" Indigo said in a furious whisper. "She will be killed if we wait any longer. I'm going to take her to the Reykjavik Aerie to keep her safe. Nobody will attack her there," He looked more exhausted than when he had first got to Carlos's place and his voice was scratchy as if his throat hurt.

"I don't know if she would be welcomed at the Aerie," Carlos countered "You heard the council leaders just now when we called them. They were quite clear that we need to follow this challenge to the end and that we can involve no one else."

Indigo snorted. "The council leaders don't understand the true danger she is in – they are old fools. Nor do I trust the prophets or the Ancestors! They have brought me nothing but pain with their omissions and their demands. They will ruin this poor girl's life and make ours miserable."

An edge of anger and bitterness seeped into my mind as Indigo's emotions flared. A small place in my mind was always aware of Indigo now, as if I had leased him some space where he could put some of his thoughts and a part of *him*. Thoughts of ocean breezes, giant birds soaring high, and a wild sense of freedom and recklessness permeated this corner of my mind as he carried on talking. Admittedly this wasn't entirely unpleasant, but it was intrusive.

I went on pretending I was asleep. I didn't like the sound of the 'poor girl' whose life was about to be ruined.

Carlos sighed, "I don't know where your mistrust comes from, Indigo, but I have faith in Pachamama. She only has the interests of all beings in her heart. Regardless of what you wish, we are here, the challenge continues, and we must protect Jasmine together."

"We have barely managed that," Indigo replied. "I nearly lost her on the ferry, and you only just got to her in time this morning when the bear attacked her. If she hadn't helped herself just now we would have lost her. Did you see? She can draw on both air and earth energy! Do you know what that means?"

"No, to be honest I have no idea! But this most recent attack does imply that we are fighting two powerful and traitorous Guardians working together – an Air and an Earth Guardian. Which is why we must work together too. I am the strongest Earth Guardian for generations. I have heard that you are one of the strongest Air Guardians, no?"

"Yes, I'm strong," said Indigo stiffly. "But it is not two Guardians, and you know that – it's Orlando. He alone can harness air and earth energy together, and all of the Air Guardians with that level of strength are too closely monitored to do this kind of harm."

Indigo's statement was met with silence and then a deep sigh.

"Even if you are right, everyone believes he died hundreds of years ago. The councillors change the subject whenever someone mentions Orlando or deny that he is still alive. I have always felt that such evil cannot truly die out. It is necessary to ensure the balance is kept."

"The balance. Hmm. Great." Indigo's voice held a hint of sarcasm. "Well, it's true that no one will believe us for now, nor will they help us. So, since you have professed your strength and might, how about you start looking for Orlando or whoever, and I will protect Jasmine."

This was too much. I sat up and spun to face them. "How about no one protects me, and you both get the hell off this island and away from me? You brought this trouble to my door, and you can take it away again."

My head throbbed with the movement. Carlos and Indigo leaped out of their seats and came to sit one on either side of me. Having them both so near was intense, and my heartbeat quickened. Both reached a hand towards me, and I raised my own to stop them.

"Oh no you don't. I'm onto that trick now. Whenever one of you touches me, it calms me like a baby and tends to make me do what you want. *You* did it on the beach, Carlos, and *you* did it several times on the ferry and in your apartment, Indigo."

Both guys had the grace to look ashamed.

"I have only ever given you comfort and release from your fear, Jasmine," said Carlos earnestly.

This was more or less true. However, Indigo had directed my thoughts away from questioning him and had me doing what he suggested with the lightest of touches on my arm.

"I am sorry, Petal. I didn't do it on purpose. Sometimes I can't control my emotion manipulation that well. It is a gift that few Guardians have, and never strongly so I have not been mentored well."

"Also. Please stay out of my head, Indigo. It's too intense … too weird. I barely know you, yet I feel like part of my mind is yours. It's making me feel schizophrenic."

"It's strange for me too, Petal. You also are taking up real estate in my head. I would not have chosen for a connection to be forged between us in this way if I had a choice, believe me. But there are things we can do to get our privacy back from each other."

I couldn't help but feel a little hurt by Indigo's wish that this hadn't happened, even if it mirrored my own, but I tried to rein in my feelings so he wouldn't notice.

"Yes," I said instead. "Please teach me that."

Carlos had moved away while I talked to Indigo. He came back and put into my hands a hot mug of something minty and earthy smelling - the stuff he had given me in the vineyard.

"I dare say you have a reaction headache from channelling air energy. What you did was amazing for someone whose abilities have only just blossomed – knocking back the attack of a very powerful Guardian. But you used a lot of strength, which is why you blacked out again. And, Jasmine, you must already know that it is too late to put the genie back in the bottle. Your trouble, and ours, is here to stay and our best chance of defeating it will be to face it together. So, we cannot let you out of our sight for now, no matter what you may think of us or our intentions."

Carlos must know how badly I had fancied both of them and was feeling sorry for me. I had no doubt that the last thing he or Indigo wanted was to be saddled with a frump like me pining after them. The last thing *I* wanted was Carlos' pity.

Indigo looked at me knowingly and I tried to clamp down on my thoughts again. I slurped at the hot drink and felt instant relief from the headache and other aches and pains I hadn't even known I had been suffering from until they were gone.

"Well, at least you're good at patching me up. That's very useful right now," I sighed.

"It is an Earth Guardian skill. Many of us specialise in healing the Earth and its inhabitants."

I stood up and walked over to the window, to get away from the intensity of feelings I experienced when Indigo and Carlos were near. I was trapped in a bad situation and anxiety was my constant companion. Even though my physical pains were gone, mental shock from the attack I had just suffered was compounding with the other recent traumas. I really needed emotional support, not just instant healing and psychic connections with strange guys from a magical race.

"Can you please lend me your phone Carlos? I need to call my friend."

Carlos looked worried but handed it over, unlocking it with a fingerprint as he did.

"It is best not to share any of this with your friends, Jasmine. They will not believe you and it will only put them in danger."

I knew this, but I needed to hear a familiar voice. My hand trembled as I took the phone from Carlos and plugged in Cherie's number, grateful that it was an easy one to remember.

Cherie answered immediately. "Jasmine? Is that you?"

I sobbed in relief at hearing her voice. It was hard work not to break down altogether.

Carlos and Indigo slipped out of the back door into the garden, giving me privacy to talk but leaving Churros and the bird to keep an eye on me.

"Cherie – how did you know it was me?"

"Well, it was an unknown number, and I was hoping. Where are you? Are you alright? Josh told me about the freaking bear!"

"So much has happened since then I don't know where to start." I took a deep breath and thought carefully. "I'm with Indigo and the guy from the other night in the vineyard. He saved me from the bear … no, not Chad!" I added when Cherie gasped. "The other one – you know?"

"Hot Hero Number One. I remember. Well, at least you're getting some action – but two guys at once! I hope you aren't getting in over your head, babe."

I grimaced. I was so far in over my head it wasn't funny. I desperately wanted to tell Cherie everything Carlos and Indigo had just told me and have her laugh it all off as ridiculous.

"It's alright, I'm alright, I think." I didn't sound convincing. "It's all a bit intense but Carlos and Indigo are the only ones who can help me right now. They think they know who is attacking me and hopefully they can stop him."

"Who are these guys, Jas? Two mysterious handsome strangers show up and protect you from awful beasts and things that go bump in the night - it's crazy! Tell me where you are and I'll come straight away. You totally need my moral support right now babe."

"Thanks, Cherie, but it's far too dangerous. Just talking to you right now has helped me more than you can imagine." It had; I felt much better for hearing her voice and grounding myself in a sense of normal life. "I've gotta go, but I'll keep you posted."

"Wait, Jas!"

I hung up before I caved and told her where I was. Carlos and Indigo reappeared seconds later, no doubt courtesy of Indigo's direct line into my thoughts. They looked expectantly at me.

I considered carefully before speaking, trying to think practically and objectively. Carlos and Indigo leaving now would not fix my problems. Someone was clearly out to get me, and I needed their help, but I also desperately wanted to take control of the situation.

"Look, I think the best thing you can do right now is to teach me how to use these Guardian powers. Then I can protect myself. I am sure there are things you'd rather do than look after me."

Indigo said nothing, but Carlos shook his head.

"I heard you talking. You both sound like you'd rather be anywhere but here, doing this ridiculous 'challenge' or whatever it is. And I'd rather you were too." I avoided looking at them as I lied and forged on assertively.

"Since you guys can't agree, Carlos can start by looking for whoever you think is attacking me, and Indigo can stay with me so we can work on getting out of each other's heads."

"Okay." Indigo smiled at me and threw a triumphant look at Carlos "I will also teach you to use the Sky Father's Andardráttur – his breath."

I didn't smile back, remembering the genocidal plan his people wanted to pursue with the help of this 'breath'.

Carlos said nothing, just took my uninjured hand and pressed it firmly to his heart which I could feel beating strongly through his thin shirt. My own heart synchronised with his and a vibration rose from below my feet, bringing with it a sense of wellbeing, belonging and, well, sheer bliss.

"This is how Earth Guardians say farewell, Jasmine. We connect with each other and Pachamama. You will be able to find me wherever I am, if you seek me out through her."

He let go of my hand and I was left alone and bereft. Wow. That was nothing short of intense and awesome, and if Carlos and Indigo were keeping score, that put Carlos one up.

Carlos turned and walked out the door with Churros at his heels.

"Wait!" I rushed after him. I didn't want him to leave, despite my intention to stay focused on my immediate problems and not let my feelings get involved.

"How will you find Orlando?"

Carlos closed his eyes and knelt down, placing hands and forehead in the grass beside the driveway. Churros lay down and placed his paws and forehead on the ground too. Carlos held out his hand and I took it, keen to see what would happen this time. I instantly felt a connection with something beneath my feet again, but even stronger now. There was the ever-present drumbeat and behind it a whispering of many voices. The object in my pocket grew warm and throbbed in time with the drum.

The voices grew louder, clamouring for my attention, until I was overwhelmed by them telling me all sorts of things that I understood intuitively but couldn't translate into words. I closed my eyes and saw a million images of nature in my mind: sunshine on outstretched leaves; rainwater flowing across roots; feet trampling on mossy ground; pebbles rolling freely down stream beds... I could sense the whole of Waiheke Island surrounding me and I saw the land as it was: a beautiful, living being clothed in sheets of green and brown. Here and there the roads and buildings interrupted the hum of it all and created silent spaces, but these places held a promise, as if nature lay dormant there and only waited for an invitation to re-emerge.

"Here, Jasmine." Carlos's voice merged with the others and pushed them back as he grabbed my awareness of the island and directed it towards the far eastern edge – an area uninhabited by people. Yet the area was utterly silent, with no murmur of nature's voices, just a sense of something ... something unfamiliar to the island's awareness.

"I will start there, I think," Carlos said as we came back to ourselves.

The voices and my awareness of the island was withdrawing and with it came a deep sense of loss that made me gasp and tear up for a moment.

Carlos stood and turned to me with something new in his eyes.

"How did you do that Jasmine? You connected with Pachamama like you have been doing it all your life! The way the island and its inhabitants welcomed you was unbelievable. I have never experienced anything like it before." He was excited, and it made him seem his age for once. He stepped close and pulled me towards him. He bent his face towards mine and I was sure he was going to kiss me.

10 THE WIND'S KISS

Indigo cleared his throat conspicuously behind us and a sting of anger and jealousy flared in the Indigo corner of my mind. Carlos stepped away from me abruptly and turned to go, glaring at Indigo as he did so.

"If you need a change of clothes or a shower, help yourself, Jasmine. There are some things you can wear in the second bedroom on the left."

With that rather welcome statement, he stalked off down the driveway with Churros frolicking at his heels. Would Carlos have kissed me if Indigo wasn't there? Would I have kissed him back or freaked out and run away?

"How will you get there?" I yelled after him with a shaky voice. "It's on the other side of the island. The bus won't take you all the way."

In answer, Carlos whistled, and a huge black horse appeared out of the trees to the right of the driveway as if it was just waiting there eagerly to be called. In one swift motion, Carlos mounted the horse. It broke into a canter and disappeared around the corner of the driveway, Churros loping alongside.

"Wow, that was beyond cool," I muttered. The sound of hoofbeats could be heard clattering up the distant lane.

"Of course, he'll just ride a horse. I don't see how he'll get there before midnight though."

"That was no ordinary horse," responded Indigo. "He has called a spirit of the forest to his aid. There shouldn't even be enough forest on this island for them to exist here, and they do not come for just anyone, even if they are an Earth Guardian." There was grudging admiration in his voice.

"Why doesn't he just drive?" I asked, although I hadn't seen a car on Carlos's property.

"No Guardian will harm the environment if they don't have to," he replied.

"How did you get here then?"

Indigo pointed to a sleek yellow motorbike near the house that I hadn't noticed with the drama of Carlos' departure.

I frowned. I hadn't heard it pull up and surely that conspicuous beast didn't conform with his comment about no Guardian harming the environment.

"It's electric, of course," said Indigo with a note of pride.

"Of course." Of course, Indigo would have a shiny, uber-cool e-motorbike. "Now about getting some privacy back in our heads…"

"Yes. If you're sure that's what you want. I'm getting used to it now if you'd rather leave it," Indigo said. Earlier he had claimed that he wanted me out of his head. I suspected he didn't want to lose whatever edge he had after witnessing Carlos and me sharing a moment.

"Come on, Petal, let's enjoy the sunshine first. It'll give us both strength."

He pointed to a bench romantically placed amidst colourful flowers, some of which I'd never seen before in my life. A trellis with vines arched over it formed a shady nook that cried out for lovers to snuggle up in it. I ignored the bench and sat on the grass opposite instead. I might be biting off more than I could chew being alone with Indigo. Carlos felt much safer, even if we had just shared a dangerous moment. Indigo sat down next to me wearing his familiar smirk and flicked his tawny gold hair over his shoulder.

"Before we begin, Indigo, let me be clear that I would *never* choose you and your genocidal people, regardless of how I might feel about either of you. And I don't", I added awkwardly, "feel anything ... anyway ... for either of you."

Indigo grinned even more widely "Come on, Petal, you can't lie or hide your feelings from me."

"Stop calling me Petal! Sure, you may have sensed what any girl might feel when someone saves their life, but I have no real romantic feelings for you at all. So, your council is going to have to give up on this stupid challenge or whatever it is."

I tried to sound firm while lying. This was difficult as I was blushing profusely. Talking this directly about romantic feelings to any boy was new and embarrassing – and it was made doubly difficult because this boy could read my thoughts and emotions.

"Okay then. Let us assume hypothetically that you have no feelings for me right now. That's not a problem, Petal, I am sure we can change that."

I ground my teeth at his statement. "Genocide, Indigo. Genocide!" His arrogance was making it easier to look him in the eye and deny any attraction.

"Ah," Indigo looked serious finally. "It's fair enough to reject me on that basis and I would myself if I were you, Petal. I can only assure you that I do not share my people's plans. There are many Air Guardians who do not. Carlos is only telling you what he knows from the council meeting where our anti-human faction spoke more loudly than anybody else."

I looked at him dubiously. "Easy enough to say."

"Yes, of course it is. But I can't lie to you through the connection the Wind's Kiss has made between us. You sense the truth of that, I know."

He moved closer and stopped with his face right in front

of mine. I flinched away – what was he doing?

"Don't worry, Petal, I'm not going to kiss you again. Yet." His grin was back. "But if you agree, I will open my mind to you, and you can read the truth in me. This is not a small thing I offer, but I can see that we won't get anywhere until you are satisfied with my intentions towards humanity."

"Okay, I guess …"

He leaned in and pressed his forehead to mine. Instantly I was overwhelmed by Indigo and his thoughts. He had been sincere about not siding with the anti-human Air Guardians. He believed that humanity could be guided to heal the Earth themselves and that no-one needed to suffer or lose their lives in the process. Behind these thoughts was an underlying anxiety, that I wouldn't accept his sincerity. Beyond that, much fainter but still detectable, was fear swirling through him: fear of failure, fear of what would happen if he won the challenge, and what would happen if he didn't, a strong sense of grief and loss that felt old but undiminished, a yearning need for acceptance from … someone … and a warm fuzzy feeling towards … who?

There was more, but thankfully he pulled away and severed the flow, then moved back from me quickly. The sense of Indigo in my mind wasn't completely gone, but his deeper emotions were hidden again. I wondered what could have caused such deep grief. It was probably his father he sought acceptance from, judging by the little I had seen of their relationship.   And who did he feel such warmth towards? A girlfriend back home perhaps.

I took a long shuddery breath. I didn't know what to say. He had bared himself to me. I didn't know if I could stand that level of honesty from anyone, let alone this strange and scarily attractive guy. Still, he had proven himself non-genocidal, which left me confused about which Guardian I would choose – should I accept that their ridiculous challenge was a going concern and play along. I wished I could talk to Cherie about it. She would have found it hysterical that I had to fall in love with someone to save the world from destruction.

"Sorry," he said earnestly, appearing more shaken than I was. "I didn't mean for you to feel *all* of that. I didn't even know that I still felt … Just give me a minute."

He strode away to the edge of the garden furthest from the driveway and the house and sank to the ground facing the ocean shimmering below. His bird swooped down from the roof of the house and landed on Indigo's shoulders, pecking gently at his ear.

To give him some privacy, I wandered away, meandering through the garden and admiring the plants and flowers. It was one of the most beautiful and strange gardens I had ever been in. Perhaps this was the influence of Carlos with his Earth Guardian skills. There was no garden like it on Waiheke that I was aware of. I stopped to admire a giant yellow sunflower, not uncommon here, but amazing in its sheer height and size. It seemed to lean towards me, and a leaf brushed my hand; with the light touch came an echo of the welcome I had experienced with Carlos when we had connected with the Earth.

I touched the bush next to the sunflower, a glossy-leafed bush with pink and yellow buds. The buds burst open with a flourish and I grinned. I turned to find the whole garden bloom and … well… open to me. Multi-coloured flowers grew from bare garden beds to full blossom in the space of seconds. Over-sized peaches, apples, quince, grapes and more ripened on vines and trees. Native trees burst out in colour next to exotic plants – glorious yellow kowhai flowers and bright red kaka-beaks contrasted with pink azaleas and giant drooping purple and blue flowers I'd never seen before. The strangest of all were giant flowers on bright green stalks that grew from nothing right next to me, surrounding me in a circle and almost touching me. The buds paused before unfolding before my eyes into tulip-like flowers in bright shades of vermillion, blue, violet, and pink. They released the most delicious scent of roses and lavender mingled together.

It was a glorious profusion of colour and life and abundance. I laughed aloud with delight and felt jasmine growing faster and more freely from my head than it had ever done before – for the first time it was in response to a happy emotion. I had never felt such uninhibited joy, as the garden welcomed me in its exuberant and bounteous way.

Finally, the garden calmed down a little. Indigo returned to our grassy knoll and stared at me with the first unguarded expression and honest smile I had ever seen on his face. I looked around self-consciously.

"Sorry, Indigo. It was insensitive of me to laugh like that when you were … well, upset about something. Are you okay now?"

"No," Indigo said. "Don't apologise for that, Petal. I have never seen an Earth Guardian work their magic, so I don't know if what you just did to this garden was normal or not, but it was beautiful to watch." He picked up a giant apple that had rolled to his feet and bit into it with a crunch.

"It's not even apple season," I said, because I didn't know what else to say. Maybe being part of this crazy story was not a bad thing after all. The connection I had with the living things around me was plain awesome! I really couldn't wait to tell Cherie about it – and Josh and Tina. They would all freak out. I couldn't help wondering what all this had to do with my biological father. But that was a mystery for another day. I had more pressing things to worry about right now.

"Anyway, where were we?" I asked as I stepped through a curtain of flowers and joined Indigo, both of us sitting cross-legged on the grass.

"Well, it's simple really. To dampen the effects of our connection you need to picture a wall around the part of your mind where you feel my presence the strongest. This will block you from sensing me, and it will also stop your thoughts and emotions leaking into my head, unless you want them to. Just then, for example, you were practically shouting "joy" and "happiness" into my head. It was … not unwelcome, especially after … well, you know." A shadow briefly passed over his face.

"Why haven't you blocked yourself from me already then?" I asked.

"I have, more or less. You've just been getting the echoes of the thoughts and feelings that I allowed out. This is all new to me, too, so I don't have perfect control of it yet. I have only ever read about it. No one of my generation has first-hand experience with the Wind's Kiss."

"I see." I wasn't sure what to think of this confession. I gave it a try, mentally building a brick wall in my mind and ring-fencing the sense of Indigo inside it. It worked instantly and easily. He was gone, just like that. Indigo looked mildly shocked and I experienced a sudden sense of loss.

"That was … effective," he said. "I don't know how you managed that so easily on your first attempt. Can you try letting me in again?"

I mentally pushed the wall over, and he was back again. Indigo had me put the wall up and down again to see if I could repeat the results. I could. He told me that we also needed to be near each other to connect and the further apart we were, the fainter the connection would be.

"You can, if you want, make a door or a window in your wall so that we can easily communicate, Petal. That does have its uses."

- Like this - I threw the words in Indigo's direction through a window in my wall. He winced, and his bird squawked in indignation.

- Yes, but not so loud! -

"How can your bird hear me too?" I asked.

"Ah, that cuts to the heart of what it is to be a Guardian, Petal. You have not yet met Arak formally. Arak. This is Jasmine. Jasmine, Arak."

Arak responded with a cry, both out loud and within the Indigo space of my mind.

"Nice to meet you, Arak."

I was rewarded with a peck on my ear.

"Now, Petal …"

 "Stop calling me Petal!" I said, without hope of a result.

True to expectation, Indigo just grinned at me. It was the grin he'd given me on the ferry. A wild sort of smile, full of dangerous promises and recklessness. I caught my breath and looked away.

Sensing his advantage, he shuffled closer, looking at me intensely as if he loved to make me uncomfortable. He sat in front of me, took my hand (such liberties these two boys took with my hands) and moved it to the pocket of my ripped and dirty pants, where the strange smooth object still rested. It started throbbing, as it had when Carlos and I had connected with the Earth.

Apparently satisfied, Indigo moved back and gave me some space. I couldn't see what this had to do with Arak, but I took the object out. Indigo beckoned to Arak. The bird flew towards him swiftly, becoming smaller and smaller and losing shape as he did so, until he fell into Indigo's palm as an object, identical in every way except colour to the one in my palm. It glowed a subtle blue and white which slowly dimmed until it looked ordinary.

"Ah," I said, marvelling. "Can mine do that too?" How cool it would be to have a companion like Churros (for this must be what Churros was to Carlos, too) or Arak.

"I don't know, to be honest. Not all Guardians have been able to draw a spirit companion from their hugskot stein – their soul stone. Not lately." Indigo went on to explain that a spirit companion is a part of your own soul that expresses itself physically and independently once you awaken to the Sky Father's breath, or to the life-force of the Earth. "Or in your case Petal, to both."

"So how many of your people have these spirit companions?" I asked.

"Maybe fifty, and there are a few thousand Air Guardians in total. As we discussed before, our abilities are waning. Of those who do have a spirit companion, many are not very strong – not like Arak or the Earth Guardian's wolf. However, I think it's likely you will be able to draw yours out, judging by the things you have already done without training."

"How do I do it then?" I asked eagerly.

"*You* don't do anything, actually. At some point, very soon I imagine, you'll fall into a spirit-awakening trance and call part of your soul out to reside in this ..." He touched my soul stone.

"Oh. That doesn't sound very useful right now!" I'd have to rely on Indigo or Carlos to protect me again while I was vulnerable and unconscious.

"Don't worry, Petal." Indigo wore his most arrogant smile. "I am here to look after you and kiss you back to life if need be."

"Indigo, did you really bring me back from the dead with a kiss?" I blurted.

His look told me everything and he reached for me. "Petal…"

I batted his hand away and stood up in case he said something that dragged me back to that night and the icy waters.

"Can we take a break? I'm really hungry and I need a shower."

Shadows were lengthening on the driveway. The summer evening light would be with us for a while yet, but it was getting late in the day.

"Of course." Indigo swept his hands towards Carlos' house as if it were his own.

The bedroom Carlos had mentioned was small and sweet with a double bed in keeping with the nautical theme: a blue bedspread with a wavy pattern. Lace curtains swayed lightly in a breeze from the open window and there was a scent of lavender throughout the room.

There was also an antique wooden cupboard with items of feminine clothing, all in my size, though a bit too refined and pastel-coloured for my taste. All of them felt and looked expensive. There was even underwear still in its packaging which was a bit weird. I selected the least delicate and fancy-looking outfit, a pair of white denim jeans and a pale blue, tailored linen shirt, and headed for the ensuite to wash off the grime from my action-packed day. I carefully put my stone ("soul stone" sounded a bit much for me) in the pocket of the clean jeans before I got in the shower, so I wouldn't forget it. If a magical spirit companion was going to emerge from it, I sure didn't want to miss that.

The shower was high pressure hot water heaven and I luxuriated for longer than I ought to have for an islander who knows how precious water is. When I finally emerged, I braided my unruly hair into a French plait (try growing through that, night-blooming jasmine!) and felt better than I had all day.

Indigo was lounging in the living room, and texting furiously. I graced him with a smile. He lifted one elegant eyebrow and put his phone down.

"That's all it takes to make you happy, Petal? A hot shower and respectable clothes?"

Deflecting the snide remark, I said brightly, "Have you found any food in the cupboard to cook? I am sure Carlos wouldn't mind."

"I am sure Carlos wouldn't mind too," he said with a sarcastic edge. "But we can do better than that. Come on. Good thing you're wearing pants, by the way." Before I could blink, he grabbed my hand and ushered me outside.

"What are you doing?" I demanded "Where are we going?!"

He didn't reply, but it was soon clear. Indigo had pulled his fancy motorbike around to the door, and before I could say lamb shanks, he had lifted me onto the back of it.

"Hang on a minute. Shouldn't we lay low? This doesn't seem sensible."

Indigo shoved a helmet at me and swung himself onto the bike in front of me, revving it as he did so. The bike didn't make a normal bike rev but made more of a high-pitched whine like a jet flying by.

"Don't worry, Petal." He was easily audible over the noise. "It'll be fine. Just go with it and stop trying to control things for a change. Hold on tight."

Control things? Me? What was he talking about? While I pondered this, he put his own helmet on, lifted his feet and accelerated down the driveway.

Unprepared, I squealed and rammed the helmet on, securing it awkwardly with one hand. I had no choice but to clasp Indigo around the waist and lean right into him. This was clearly a misguided attempt to seduce me. As if the feel of his taut muscular chest through thin layers of clothing would do that. I moved my thoughts away from this chest and drew on a well of outrage at him for railroading me. Had he asked, I would have told him I wasn't getting on his motorbike because they're just not safe. I've heard of way too many horrible accidents. We didn't even have protective leathers.

"Wait!" I yelled as we stopped briefly at the driveway exit. "I didn't agree to this and I don't think it's a good idea."

Indigo took no notice, and we shot off down the road as if we didn't have a care in the world.

11 A DATE WITH DISASTER

Riding a motorbike on a warm summer evening was nothing short of heaven. I forgot everything and simply enjoyed the moment. The speed gave me a rush, and I even let myself enjoy the feeling of holding a boy close, ephemeral though it might be. We headed down quiet back lanes overlooking the ferry harbour until we met the main road which ran along the island's ridge.

Soon we were in the countryside, far from Waiheke's town centre and urban areas. I breathed in the fresh air and felt the wind pulling at me, calling to me to let go and fly free. For a moment I almost did, but common sense made me cling tighter to Indigo instead.

Indigo slowed down way too soon. We turned down a red dirt driveway near the western end of Waiheke and through beautiful oak gates that bore the sign, 'Pukeko Bay Vineyard and Bistro'. Ah yes, this would be Indigo's style. I'd never had reason to come here, but Cherie had worked here as a waitress last summer and told me all about it. It was a gorgeous place and very upmarket.

We cruised slowly down the driveway and pulled up in front of a long steel and glass building just as the sun began to set. Through the huge open doors, we could see the terrace on the other side and the sweeping lawn in front of it that boasted a sculpture garden. The fading light glinted off the colourful frames of several kinetic sculptures. Indigo parked beside an ornate shrubbery at the side of the entrance. I was sure it wasn't an actual park, but he didn't seem to care as he, dismounted and turned to help me off. Freed from the enchantment of the ride, I ignored his hand.

"For crying out loud, Indigo. We didn't even have protective clothing!" My complaint was undermined by the ferocious grin on my face and the happy afterglow from the ride.

"We don't need that, Petal. We are Air Guardians! Just ask and the wind will catch you. Didn't you hear it calling to you back there? Besides, you loved it. Tell me you didn't. Wait until you learn to ride the wind itself."

A concierge rushed down the steps towards us, feet crunching in the white pebbles of the turning bay.

"Hey you can't park your bike there kids… Omigod, is that an electric BeeX! I didn't know they were even on the market yet, let alone in New Zealand! How did you get it with yellow trimmings? Is it yours? Can I sit on it?"

Indigo laughed. "It's a prototype and sure you can. Do you want me to take your photo?"

Five minutes later, Indigo left his motorbike parked right where it was. No doubt it would add to the aura of glamour that the bistro wanted to promote. It certainly added to Indigo's appeal as the concierge handed us over to the hostess. I was having doubts again about this trip. We were not keeping a low profile here. But Indigo was sweeping me along as he whispered something in the hostess' ear and handed her a card. She smiled back at him, charmed, but also asked for his ID to prove he was over eighteen. I caught a glimpse of his passport as he flashed it - he was nearly 19 according to the document. Despite his youth, he acted with the assertiveness of someone used to people saying yes – perhaps that came with being super rich, as he obviously was.

"Of course, come right this way."

I hoped the hostess didn't recognise me. Several years ago, she'd babysat me a few times. Right now, she only had eyes for Indigo and I wasn't wearing the usual Waiheke Island teenager outfit so maybe she wouldn't recognise me.

We were led past the terrace packed with diners enjoying the spectacular view of the sculptures and Auckland city in the distance across the water. I wondered where we were going, until the hostess led us down some stairs to a door labelled 'Private Dining'. It opened to a room with two long dark tables and an extensive wine cellar behind a glass wall.

Ambient music filled the room, a haunting voice singing of love and loss. Romantic lighting came from an ornate chandelier that provided an interesting contrast to the sleek modern fit-out, which was all concrete, steel and glass. I couldn't accuse Indigo of having a hidden agenda as it was pretty obvious what he was trying to do here. He was wining and dining me because he was out to win, regardless of the doubts he had expressed earlier about the Sky Father and his challenge. Mild disgust at his intentions and the decadence of the private dining room roiled through me, and I lowered my mental wall so he could sense this. My parents had instilled in me a sense that it was wrong to flaunt wealth around the way that Indigo was. It was also hypocritical of Indigo's people if they did mean to save the planet from environmental apocalypse.

- We do need to be a bit discreet, Petal, and money can buy that. Also, I just want to see you have a good time; I have no ulterior motives -

The hostess settled us in and went to get menus and table settings. I felt nervous in the fancy surrounds and started fidgeting with the fork.

"This is your idea of discreet! Really? This is a small island, Indigo. Probably my first-grade primary school teacher and her aunt know we're here by now. And don't try to fool me about your motives. I'm not completely naïve, dude."

I slammed my mental wall up again. Talking mind-to-mind was just too intimate.

"You could sense the truth of my intentions if you wanted to, Petal. Just relax for a bit. You might enjoy yourself."

The hostess returned with menus and poured us expensive-looking sparkling water. She gave me a curious look as she did so. I could see she was struggling to recall who I was. She turned to Indigo and asked what wine he'd like and then she recited the list of specials. I was annoyed to be ignored in favour of Indigo, but he was clearly the one in control here so I could hardly blame her. Indigo rose to the occasion, ordering food and wine for us both and flirting shamelessly with the hostess as he did so. I sat back and glared at him for no good reason (okay, maybe the flirting made me jealous) but he ignored my sour looks.

"I don't drink alcohol, Indigo. I'm only seventeen," I said when the hostess had gone.

He raised his elegant brow. "We are not drinking alcohol to get drunk like a couple of teenagers enjoying their first alco-pops, Petal. One glass of wine is a perfectly acceptable with any meal, particularly as they have carefully matched food and wine. Or so the hostess told me."

I still doubted his intentions and found his comments patronising, but when the wine came with the meal, I took a sip. I didn't regret it; the wine brought out the flavours in the food. Indigo had ordered the vegan set menu and it was delicious. I found myself relaxing despite everything and enjoying myself in Indigo's company.

We both avoided talk of Guardians, the challenge or anything else controversial. Off these topics and away from Carlos, his father, and the wait staff, Indigo's arrogance disappeared, and he was fun to be with. He told me about his home in Iceland and his travels to interesting places around the world. He was light on personal details and didn't mention his family at all, but I wasn't surprised given my earlier insight into his emotions. I let my guard down and laughed at his amusing anecdotes, wishing I could see some of the places he described with such enthusiasm. Although I had always considered myself a homebody, he made travel sound like great fun.

Somehow, one glass of wine became two and I found myself opening up and telling him about my life on Waiheke, my parents and how confused and angry I was about my mother's failure to tell my dad or me the truth about my biological father.

"I mean, what was she thinking? My dad had every right to be angry at her and I can't really forgive her either."

"I have a thought about that, Petal. Your mum may not be as much to blame as you think." He looked at me as my confusion cleared and I realised what he was suggesting. It really was unlikely that Mum would lie to Dad about something that important. Someone may have manipulated her using Guardian powers, as Carlos and Indigo had done when calming me down or getting me to do what they wanted.

- Yes - Indigo said in my mind - it's possible that a very strong Guardian could put a suggestion on her, telling her not to say anything to anyone about your father. She would have had to be a little receptive to the idea, though, for it to stick for this long -

"I suppose she deserves a hearing, at least," I sighed. If my biological father was half as charming or attractive as Carlos or Indigo, it wouldn't have been hard for my mother to fall for him. I needed to talk to Mum to see what else she knew about all of this.

"Don't hold a grudge against your loved ones, Petal." Indigo distracted me from my thoughts, suddenly intense again. "You never know when they will be taken from you."

The hidden well of grief I'd sensed earlier when he opened his mind to me was back in evidence, although more contained. This time, I could read it in his face and eyes. What another might mistake for coldness and disdain was Indigo hiding his pain.

I shifted a bit closer and placed my hand on his. He breathed a bit unsteadily and turned his hand over, clasping mine tightly.

"What happened, Indigo? Who did you lose?" I asked carefully.

Indigo ignored my question. "You are the most extraordinary person I have ever met, Jasmine. You completely disarm me." He let down his cold mask and behind it was a dangerous look that sent chills up my spine.

He leaned in close to me and I knew he was going to try and kiss me. I … well … I turned my face to his and let him. I could have blamed the wine, or his ability to manipulate me, or even his impossible physical beauty. It was none of these things. I simply wanted to know what it would be like.

It was amazing. He tasted of spices and wine and … but I don't need to describe it. If you've ever been kissed thoroughly, you'll know what it was like. It was far, far superior to the bumbling, awful kiss Chad had forced on me. It was also too short because we were interrupted by a waiter knocking discreetly at the door to clear our plates and ask if we wanted dessert.

Indigo pulled away and I blushed fiercely and looked down at the table. We both muttered a hasty response and the waiter left with a knowing look. Indigo looked at me without quite meeting my eyes, then he drew himself up and put on his arrogant smile again, like armour.

"I didn't think I would enjoy this challenge as much as I am," he said, and I flinched. I could have hit him for reminding me of what I really was to him, and for ruining that wonderful kiss. I was nothing more than a prize to be won, then tossed aside for a new adventure or experience.

Indigo's face fell as he saw the impact his words had on me, and a lone flower dislodged from my head to fall in front of us like an accusation.

There was no time to say more, though. The door swung open and Cherie swept into the room, with Josh and Tina close behind. She took in my proximity to Indigo, my red face and slightly swollen lips, and I knew that she could tell exactly what had happened. I scraped my chair back and crossed my arms. Cherie made no comment, and Josh and Tina were too late to witness what she had.

"Woah, how did you guys find us here?" I had a fair idea. I cringed at how guilty I sounded, as if I was hiding something. Which I was. Quite a lot.

"My sister's ex-boyfriend's cousin saw you and Indigo coming here and texted me," Cherie said. "She's the hostess here, and all the staff wanted to know who Indigo is."

Indigo took this as a compliment, and the arrogant grin returned. I sighed, even though I knew it was just a mask he wore most of the time. Argh, he was so complicated. I had always promised myself never to get involved with complicated people and here I was, neck deep in them.

"Jas, I was super worried after you called me, so I asked everyone I knew on the island to look out for you. I can see I was right to worry." She looked meaningfully at Indigo.

"Islands," he said with disdain. "I should have known."

I glared at him, itching to say *I told you so* or remind him that he was also from an island.

Cherie and Josh helped themselves to seats at the table. I had to admit I was glad to see them. It was a relief to be rescued from the situation with Indigo.

"You don't mind if we join you, do you." Josh said with a glare in Indigo's direction. He then turned straight to me. "Jas, your parents are worried sick. After the bear, we didn't know what had happened to you! I was out with Duncan scouring the streets when I got Cherie's call that you were here. And here you are living it up at the swankiest vineyard on the island with *him*. What's got into you? The Jasmine I know would never be this reckless and irresponsible."

"Josh, my parents don't know where I am, do they?" He was right, and I was ashamed of myself for letting Indigo sweep me up into his date night plan when I should have been laying low to protect both myself and my family and friends from whoever was stalking me. Now my friends had been sucked into my dangerous problems again.

"No. Not yet."

I sighed in relief.

"We wanted to give you a chance to explain."

Indigo had been sitting back watching with his arms folded, but now he stood up abruptly.

"Petal, we should go. If your friends can find us, so can others. You should all leave as well." He looked at my friends. "There is much more going on here than you know and just being around Jasmine right now puts you all in great danger. As you have already experienced."

Josh bristled, and Cherie looked ready to disagree. Before anyone could say anything else, Indigo swayed on his feet and sat down again with a strange look on his face.

"What ... it must be the wine." Then a look of horror came over his face. He looked directly at me. "Petal! I'm so sorry. I've been an idiot. Get out of here!" he said as he collapsed.

Tina shrieked and rushed to stop him as slipped off the seat and onto the concrete floor. He was too heavy, though, and they both landed in a heap just as the door opened and somebody entered. I couldn't see who as my vision was growing hazy and my head heavy and I knew that I was also about to pass out the same way Indigo had.

"Who the hell are you?" Cherie's asked, her voice assertive but clearly afraid.

The last thing I heard was the reply - it sent a chill of terror through me.

"I am Orlando, my dear. The Earth Mother's last and best hope against the scourge of humanity."

12 ORLANDO

I woke in a dark, grim little concrete room where a single glowing bulb dangled from the ceiling. The floor was wet, the air damp and cold. I was lying on a camp stretcher set against the wall opposite the only exit, a rusty iron door. I couldn't think how I'd come to be here. The only thing I could grasp was that my head was pounding fiercely.

Slowly memory returned and I cringed inwardly as I remembered how Indigo and I had kissed. Then everything after the kiss came flooding back and I froze. Orlando had me! Possibly my friends and Indigo too. I panicked and leapt up, banging on the door, and yelling when it wouldn't open. I persisted until my voice went hoarse and my fists were sore, but no-one came. I sank down onto the stretcher and hugged my knees, nursing my head, the ache not improved by exertion. Flowers sprouted from my head in an unstoppable cascade.

I was locked in a kind of dungeon. I could die here. And what about my friends? Panic rose and swiftly overwhelmed me. *I could feel the icy grip of cold dark waters pulling me down to oblivion.*

Without Carlos, Indigo or Tina to help me, I spiralled into a terrifying, breathless place where every moment I was sure my heart would burst. Dread pinned me to the stretcher with my knees hugged tight to my chest as I moaned and cried for what seemed like hours. Finally, the attack abated, and I lay wrung out and limp. I could do nothing but stare at the ceiling surrounded by the flowers that had finally stopped growing out of my head.

Minutes stretched into hours with nothing happening and only silence for company. I tried to reach Indigo in my mind, but there was no sound or sense of him whatsoever.

Boredom replaced fear as my headache abated. I avoided dwelling on the danger my friends and I were in. I chose to think calm positive thoughts to avoid another panic attack and started to take stock of my situation. I wasted time berating myself for giving in to Indigo's reckless impulse. I had known that we should have stayed in the relative safety of Carlos' house.

I had to admit to myself that I had been having one of the best nights of my life before Orlando showed up. It was my first-ever date (even if it wasn't real to Indigo, it was to me) and an amazing one as far as I could tell. Well, amazing until Indigo ruined it by reminding me of his real agenda in taking me out - the Guardians' stupid challenge. And the whole experience had cost too much; my friends were in danger now because of my recklessness. I needed to know if they were safe.

At least I had a fairly good idea where I was. This room must be part of the tunnel network at Stony Batter. I'd been here on school trips and with friends. Kids also came here when they were skipping school, to do all sorts of things. I'd never enjoyed exploring the maze of narrow tunnels and rooms. The place was creepy and claustrophobic.

For some reason I couldn't remember, the tunnels were closed to the public right now, which was probably why Orlando could hide out here undetected.

There was a ray of hope. This was where Carlos had been headed when I last saw him. Through our connection with the Earth, we'd sensed something here that was unfamiliar to the island' atmosphere. I kicked myself, remembering; I could connect with the Earth as I had in Carlos' Garden. I put my hand to the cold wall. For several frustrating minutes, I felt nothing. Maybe I needed direct contact with the Earth, but that wasn't possible in this concrete bunker. I concentrated harder, seeking any sign of life anywhere – but there was nothing. This might be why Orlando had imprisoned me here. Cut off from the natural world, my newfound abilities were of no use.

I tried again to reach Indigo. I threw open all the doors and windows in the wall I had built between Indigo and myself. This time, in the Indigo corner of mind, I sensed a faint impression of sunshine and storm-tossed ocean waves. Relief flooded me. At least he was alive, which gave me hope for Cherie, Josh and Tina as well.

My stomach was rumbling, and I was desperate to pee when I heard footsteps and snuffling from the tunnel outside the room. The door swung open with a loud bang and a middle-aged man stepped through, followed closely by the giant bear that had attacked me in my bedroom and the leshy. The leshy had obviously survived its dunking in the waters between Waiheke and Auckland.

Despite the leshy's creepy glare and the bear's menacing growling, it was Orlando who scared me the most. He was an ordinary-looking man of average height and build. He wore jeans and a lightweight grey sweater with sneakers, the classic look of an American tourist. His defining features were a long face and huge brown eyes. I couldn't put my finger on why he was creeping me out so much. Maybe it was the way he was staring at me with those large eyes, as if I was a strange specimen he was about to dissect. Or maybe it was his slow accent-free drawl.

"Hush, Hugo." He touched the bear lightly on the nose. 'Hugo' fell silent and sat back on his haunches, giving Orlando an affectionate nuzzle. Just as Churros and Arak did with Carlos and Indigo. The leshy lurched around the bear and dumped a empty bucket and a plate of bread and cheese on the ground in front of me before leaving.

"Jasmine, welcome. I apologise for my previous attempts to introduce myself. You must have thought I was trying to kill you when I sent Hugo and my leshy after you. Actually, I was ... but of course, after I experienced your power when you rejected my tornado yesterday, I knew I had made a serious mistake."

His friendly smile was contradicted by the scary voice. Had I met him under different circumstances I scarcely would have noticed him, let alone been afraid, but for some reason he was causing me terror just by looking at me.

"Where are my friends? What did you do to them? If you've hurt them, so help me, I'll…"

I was stopped by a growl from the bear and a frown from Orlando as he placed a hand on my arm. A wave of fear swept over me. I stepped back and stumbled into the stretcher.

"Your friends are all fine … for now. Let's focus on more important matters." He drew himself up and spoke in a grandiose manner that would have been ridiculous if I wasn't so scared of him.

"I am Orlando. You may have heard of me from your foolish Guardian acquaintances."

Wow, no last name – just Orlando. As if he was a rock star. This guy was clearly short of a few chips, as Mum would say.

"My dear Jasmine, now that I am aware of how powerful and interesting you are, I would never harm *you*, because we are alike. We are special."

I drew upon anger at my situation and the way he had threatened my friends to push away fear. It was easier than it should have been, and I realised that he had been manipulating my emotions to make me afraid of him.

"We are *not* alike. I don't go around attacking innocent people. I don't know what issues you have with the Guardians, but they're nothing to do with me."

He laid his hand on me again and a fresh wave of fear

left me helpless and silent despite my knowledge of the manipulation he was using on me.

"I have already apologised for the earlier misunderstanding between us, Jasmine. I won't do so again."

He started to rant on about how amazing and auspicious our meeting was. He claimed that we were the only Guardians alive that were directly descended from both the Sky Father and the Earth Mother, and that I was the first such Guardian to be born for generations.

"Together, Jasmine, you and I can be the most powerful beings on this planet!" He had taken his hand off me at some point, and the debilitating fear receded.

"Great. You're just as nutty as the rest of the Guardians." I muttered and then started to giggle a bit hysterically. Orlando was such a clichéd power-hungry villain.

Orlando leaned forward and slapped me hard.

I fell back onto the bed, clutching my face in shock – no one had ever hit me before. Okay, he was kind of ridiculous, but also violent and dangerous. I had to keep it together if I wanted to get out of here unharmed.

Orlando carried on as if nothing had happened. "I admit that at first I saw you as simply a tool of the prophets. If I had let the challenge run unhindered, those foolish young Guardians would ruin everything and have all the power that should rightfully be mine. But that was before I saw your potential. Let me teach you and together we can heal the Earth, without any prophecies or challenges."

"You don't care about the world. You want nothing but power!" I burst out and then cringed, waiting for another blow.

Orlando didn't hit me this time. He gave me his creepy smile.

"You are right that I like power. Why shouldn't I? Do you know what the prize is that the Sky Father and Earth Mother offer to the winner of their ridiculous challenge to win your affections?"

Indigo and Carlos had given me a vague notion about the prize: power of some kind, but that's all I knew. I said nothing.

Orlando guessed my predicament. "No doubt your Guardian suitors don't want you to know what the winner of the challenge stands to gain. Their entire clan's powers would be restored to the level of the first descendants and the winner himself would be the most powerful Guardian who has ever lived."

My heart fell. Carlos had alluded to this, but I hadn't wanted to think about it. Indigo and Carlos would probably do anything for that prize. They both talked with such passion about their clans and the way they were diminishing in power. So that was the goal of Indigo's amazing date and kiss, and of Carlos's kindness and care. It was all a deception. They didn't have feelings for me. How could they? They barely knew me and even if they did ... well, regardless, they wanted to deceive me and win the challenge.

Orlando could sense he was making an impact. I've never been good at hiding my feelings, and I wasn't trying to now. I didn't care. Despite knowing better, I'd let feelings develop for both Indigo and Carlos.

"You see, they are no better than me, Jasmine. They are just after power, too. At least I am being honest and not trying to do something as deceitful as make you fall in love with me."

I looked away in embarrassment, my face flaming. He could see how pathetic it was for me to think that Indigo or Carlos might return my feelings.

"I've given you a lot to think about. I'm sorry that I can't move you to more hospitable accommodation to do that thinking in. This is the only concrete bunker I have available currently, and I haven't had time to make it more comfortable. However, I have seen to your needs." He smiled and waved magnanimously in the direction of the bucket and the plate of food.

I remained silent and he dropped his smile to look at me frostily.

"You *will* thank me later, Jasmine. If there is one thing I can't stand, it is ingratitude. It's such a Guardian trait."

With that he twirled – yes, he twirled as if he was wearing a cape, not a v-neck sweater and sneakers – and swept out of the room. Hugo gave a last menacing growl in my direction and stalked after him. The door slammed behind them with a resounding bang.

I let out a breath I didn't know I'd been holding and leaned against the wall. What he had told me about the 'prize' rang true. I was angry all over again with Carlos, Indigo, all of the ridiculous Guardians I had never met, and the Earth Mother and Sky Father, conceptual as they might be. It was not cool of them to play with my emotions like this. Not cool.

Now was the time to harden my heart and think my way out of this mess so I could get rid of Orlando *and* Indigo and Carlos. All I wanted in that moment was for everything to go back to the way it had been a week ago, when I was just a normal teenage girl looking forward to a long uncomplicated summer hanging out with my friends at the beach.

None of these thoughts stopped me from wolfing down the meagre meal the leshy had brought for me. I wasn't one to hold back from food because my enemy had given it to me. Even if he had recently drugged my wine. Well, that thought made me pause, but I couldn't do much about it now. Nor did any principle stop me from using the bucket because I was desperate. I lay down again and tried to calm my inner emotional turmoil by singing love ballads to myself. Also, to prove to myself and Orlando that I wasn't emotionally destroyed by his words. I wasn't!

Cherie always laughs at me when I sing eighties love songs, but it makes me feel better when I'm down. They weren't a good choice this time though, and I let the words fade away as they became a bit raw, and I realised what many of the love songs were trying to say for the first time. I'd never really needed anyone before (except my parents in the usual way). Now, much as I tried to deny it, I needed Carlos and Indigo in the worst possible way, and it hurt badly that they were playing games with me to achieve their own goals. I switched to some rap music to perk myself up and it made me smile in defiance for a moment, but then I felt no better. I was emotionally destroyed after all.

I got out my soul stone and stroked it, hoping it would soothe me as it had before. I put it straight down when it became uncomfortably hot and started glowing brightly. It was mesmerizing, and I couldn't look away. A shape was struggling within it, wriggling and squirming like a chick trying to break out of an egg. As I leaned close to see what it was, a wave of heat pulsed over my body and the light blinded me. I felt myself lift into the air and float freely in a warm and light bubble.

Looking down, I saw receding from me, a pale, scruffy girl with dirty hair and clothes. Her eyes were closed as she lay on a camp stretcher in a dark barren room. It took me a moment to appreciate that this girl was me. I could only watch as she/I grew further and further away. A great sense of calm and peace came over me as I slipped down a tunnel of light, away from my body and its cold prison cell.

13 MY SPIRIT COMPANION IS AWESOME

If this was death, it was far more peaceful than near-drowning had been. I could still feel the cold air on my skin, though, and the various aches and pains I'd collected recently. So perhaps I wasn't dying even if I was no longer in my body.

Eventually, warmth and peace completely cocooned and cut me off from my physical body. All that had happened recently made sense in this peaceful state and I finally accepted my strange new existence.

With acceptance came the understanding that the revelations of the past few days had been threatening my sense of identity. I saw myself as a normal, slightly bookish teenager, who liked to hang out with friends and didn't need excitement. All this magic, danger and drama was not something I was attracted to. No wonder I'd been so anxious and needy with Carlos after the bear attack, and so receptive to Indigo' charms. I was confused and vulnerable.

I let myself relax and float in this state of endless warmth and self-understanding. Ah, how Cherie would laugh when I tried to describe this; she'd think I was turning into my mum. Eventually it dawned on me that Indigo had warned me that I might fall into a spirit-awakening trance. What bad timing. Just when I needed all my senses alert to escape Orlando, here I was, lying unconscious in his possession. It was hard to be fearful in the cocoon though, and my worries kept slipping away as soon as I reached for them.

Eventually, I noticed movement at the corner of my vision. Someone or something was here with me. Maybe they'd been here all along. I looked carefully about and could make out a small shape fluttering around me, its edges blurred with rainbow colours, as if I was seeing it though a prism.

When the shape noticed me noticing it, it gave a shriek of joy and launched itself at me. Even though I wasn't in my physical body, it managed to crash into me and send me reeling back down the tunnel of light, away from the cosy cocoon. I struggled, not wanting to re-enter my traumatised body but I couldn't avoid it and slammed painfully into my physical form. It hurt in so many places and was so heavy and fleshy. The calm I'd experienced in the spirit-awakening trance was gone. I was back to heightened anxiety, mind and heart racing at the reality of my situation.

Something positive stayed with me, though. I knew who I was now, who I had always been. I was Jasmine, a girl from Waiheke Island. But I was also connected to something strange and wonderful in a way that I was beginning to accept and even welcome. I was powerful and unique, even if I didn't feel worthy of it yet.

I'd also been left with a surprisingly heavy kitten-sized creature sitting on my chest. It had the head and breast of a gold-and-brown-flecked eagle and the golden flanks of a lion. Its two halves blended perfectly, and it had wings folded behind it. Sparkling ruby-coloured eyes looked at me expectantly. Before I could process any of this, there was a creaking noise beside me. I turned to see Orlando sitting next to me in a plush armchair.

"Marvellous, Jasmine. Marvellous! You have a griffin

for a spirit companion. That is a first for any Guardian. The ancestors have a sense of appropriateness, after all. Air and earth elements mingled in one creature."

"How long have I been … out of it?" I asked groggily "and how long have you been sitting there watching me?" *You creep,* I kept myself from adding.

The griffin on my chest had no such restraint. It rose to its full height with spread wings and hissed at Orlando ferociously. Its wings were magnificent, as wide as its body was long, and tawny with flecks of red and violet.

Orlando glared at the little creature, and it subsided a bit, folding its wings gracefully behind it.

"The griffin reflects your true emotions, Jasmine. What have I done to make you angry? But in answer to your question, you have been in your spirit-awakening trance for two days. I was beginning to think I might have to force you out of it before you found your Spirit Companion. You are powerful enough without one."

"Two days!" I sat up in alarm and dislodged my little companion. It squawked indignantly and snuggled into my side instead. Its presence gave me comfort and made me less afraid as I faced Orlando.

"You have to let me go. My mum and dad will be so worried about me, and the police will be looking everywhere!"

"Actually, you don't have to worry about your parents and the police, Jasmine. Or your friends. I have led them all to believe that you have gone to a soccer camp on the mainland."

"Soccer! That's ridiculous. I don't do any sports besides surfing and sailing. I especially hate team sports like soccer. They'll never go for it. Nor will Indigo and Carlos…"

I stopped. The two Guardians would be looking for me to help fulfil their challenge, but did I want them to find me? Whatever acceptance of my Guardian powers I'd achieved in the trance, it hadn't taken away the pain of knowing that Indigo and Carlos couldn't care less about me except as a pathway to power.

"Don't you worry about any of it, Jasmine. I'll take care of it all. You can leave your old life behind you soon anyway. You have me and her, that's all you need." He nodded at the griffin.

"Her…?"

"Yes, you are a female and so is your Spirit Companion, of course. I'll send in some refreshments while I go and prepare for travel. We will leave this place soon and then you won't have to be bothered by the Guardians ever again."

"Leave? No! I don't want to leave, and especially not with you. My life is here. My family is here and … I know who I am. I don't need your help to be that person."

I didn't want to be taken away from Waiheke, away from my life. I missed my parents fiercely in that moment and let go of any anger I had against Mum. Now I knew how manipulative Guardians were, I didn't blame her at all. I blamed my biological father who was probably a Guardian.

"Hush, my dear. You do need me although you don't know it yet, and in time we will be partners." Orlando stood up as he said this and headed for the door where he paused briefly.

"Oh, and don't try anything with your griffin yet, Jasmine. She is young and weak, and you could easily harm her or yourself if you overdo it. I would hate to have to … clip her wings."

With this veiled threat he left me and closed the door. I looked at my strange new companion with a flare of concern at the thought of anything harming her, though I'd only known her for five minutes. She was a piece of my soul after all.

A few minutes after Orlando left, the leshy came and left me with food and water. It was a much more appetising and substantial meal than last time: vegetable stew with lentils and fresh bread. I was so hungry I practically inhaled it. My griffin showed no interest in food. Instead, she wandered around our concrete prison inspecting various points of interest with a serious air. When she came to the door, she leapt up to the lock, shoved her beak into it, and fidgeted for a few minutes. When she leapt back again, the door swung open of its own accord. My clever griffin! Minutes in existence and she had already proved herself a griffin of action.

I jumped up and rushed out the door, with no thought for Orlando or his threat to take my griffin away. I wasn't going to sit around waiting for him to do his worst. No, if my griffin was a woman of action then so was I.

The tunnel outside my room stretched away dark and empty. I ran down the corridor with my griffin flapping excitedly a metre or two ahead. Several turns later, we were in complete darkness, the light from my room vanished behind us. I ran my hand down the wall choosing the left turn at every juncture. None of the tunnel complexes on Waiheke were very big or complex. Eventually we would find an exit.

Several minutes later, I failed to respond to my griffin's warning peep and ran straight into a wall. Putting a hand to my head, I felt blood and a painful lump. A new injury to add to my collection. Sighing, I felt around carefully and found that we had come to a dead end, but there was a metal rung ladder set into the wall, heading upwards. Most likely this was one of the exits to the old gun emplacements. Many were blocked by trapdoors kept permanently closed to stop people falling into the long shafts beneath. I remembered Josh and Cherie climbing a similar ladder last time we visited the tunnels, whooping in the darkness as they daringly turned their torches off a long way above Tina and me. There was no escape this way.

A roar echoed through the tunnel behind us. It was Orlando's bear and he sounded mad. My absence had been discovered. I reached for the wall to steady myself as a wave of dread rose and threatened to reduce me to a whimpering mass on the ground. This was no time for a panic attack.

A soft feathery touch on my hand and a comforting feeling in my mind brought me back to myself.

I clenched my fists against the dirt of the wall. Dirt! Feeling around, I found that a section of the concrete wall had cracked apart, exposing the damp ground around it. This was why they had closed the tunnels, I remembered. There had been some dangerous collapses. It was helpful to me now though as I sent my awareness out into the surrounding earth with a wordless plea for help. I sensed a brief and faint response, but I couldn't stick around and commune with nature. Orlando's bear was tearing down the corridors, after us.

The griffin gently pecked my hand and we set off back the way we'd come trailing my hand along the wall carefully. I soon came across an opening that I had missed before and turned into it, heading away from the bellowing bear. Only the griffin at my side kept me from despairing in the dark as the bear's panting and growling grew closer. He was nearly upon us when we burst out into a bright tunnel – daylight! A short tunnel's length lay between us and freedom. Right behind us, Hugo was rounding the corner, the leshy and Orlando not far behind. The leshy's distinctive hissing could be heard over the bear's grunts and roars. Possibly this was because there were now three leshys. Orlando held up his hand and his merry little band of followers stopped metres away.

Orlando strode towards me grimly. "Disappointing, Jasmine, disappointing. There is no way out for you, my dear, and I'm afraid your little companion is going to suffer for your ingratitude." He stopped beside me, a mad glint in his eye.

There was no way I could escape him now, without access to the natural environment. Or even Carlos and Indigo. I'd gratefully take help from them at this point.

- Petal, hold on! We're nearly there -

I sobbed with relief, hearing Indigo in mind. Arak echoed his thoughts, and not far off a wolf howled but I tried not to look anything less than dejected as Orlando grabbed my arm.

My griffin leaped at Orlando, screeching and attacking. Orlando slapped her to the ground with a strength that belied his body and she lay there dazed and unmoving. I tried to pull away, but Orlando's unnatural strength held me pinned. A figure darkened the tunnel entrance and I heard Carlos yell my name.

Orlando narrowed his eyes in anger as Carlos and Churros charged up the tunnel towards us. He started to drag me towards his hoard of creepy helpers. Before we reached them, the tunnel around us erupted in a shower of dirt and rocks, and the ground shook violently. I was thrown down and surrounded by hordes of little people no higher than my knee.

"Gnomes!" Orlando shrieked as he fended off at least thirty of the small people. They were beautiful to look at, with skin in various shades of brown, gold, and white and long multi-coloured hair falling to their waists. I stared as they swarmed over Orlando and his crew. A ferocious battle ensued, with the gnomes brandishing long wooden poles and overwhelming their opponents by sheer force of numbers. It was tight quarters for a fight and the little people clearly had the advantage. The leshys and the bear were flailing around, whacking their limbs on the tunnel walls, and Orlando was similarly disadvantaged.

Hugo freed himself with a massive roar. He leaped towards me as I lay prone on the ground trying to drag myself away from the battle and towards my little griffin who was barely visible beneath debris and dirt. Something seemed to be wrong with my leg and I couldn't move it. A slab of broken concrete had fallen, pinning my leg beneath it. I stared at the bear, unable to stand up and face it.

I didn't have to. Churros leapt over me and threw himself at Hugo, just as he had on the beach. Then Carlos was on his knees beside me. He touched my shoulder, and a shot of strength flooded into me, relieving some of the pain from my injuries.

"Can you move Jasmine?"

"No. My leg's trapped. My Spirit Companion! Please help her. She's over there." I pointed, and Carlos looked at where my griffin lay, starting in surprise when he saw her little form.

"A griffin," he said with awe. "I have never heard of such a spirit animal!" He turned away and whistled sharply.

A small faction of our allies left the battle and headed over to us. Up close, they were indeed beautiful. There were only ten and I couldn't imagine what use such small people would be until together they grabbed the broken section of concrete and whisked it effortlessly off my leg. Without hesitation they lifted me and raced me along the tunnel towards the daylight.

"Carlos. What's going on? My griffin!"

"Do not worry, Jasmine! She is coming."

He was right. Another group of little people were carrying the still form of my griffin. They caught up to us and unceremoniously dumped her on my chest before turning and heading back into the fierce battle behind us.

"I will be with you shortly," Carlos yelled over the din as I was drawn helplessly away, and he went to join the battle.

"No, Carlos!" I shouted, although I don't know what I was trying to achieve. He wasn't likely to listen to me. I longed for a familiar face, rather than the strange silent people carrying me.

The universe provided. The little people dumped me at the exit, then dived into the ground as if it were a swimming pool; I watched as their kicking legs disappeared. Indigo was waiting right outside the tunnel entrance.

"Petal!" he said. "Thank the heavens! I was about to come in. Air Guardians do not go well underground, but I was honestly about to come in anyway. Wait, is that a griffin?"

I looked at him with mild disgust, but not because of his apparent claustrophobia. I couldn't blame him for that. In any case, Carlos and his strange friends had it all under control.

Out of the tunnel and away from Orlando, I was aware again of Carlos and Indigo's deceitfulness. The last time I saw Indigo, he had kissed me to win a competition.

"Don't worry, Indigo, Carlos has it in hand."

Indigo's face turned sour. He drew himself up and charged into the tunnel. Arak flapped around the entrance, screeching and throwing accusing looks at me, but unable to enter without hitting his wings on the walls. I dragged myself and my griffin under a tree out, of the hot sun.

Whatever happened in the tunnel, I couldn't run away. I would stand my ground here in the open. Actually, I'd have to sit my ground as I couldn't stand on my damaged leg. It was such a relief to be out of those cold dark tunnels. I turned my attention to my poor little griffin, relieved to find her warm and breathing although still unconscious.

As the minutes ticked by, I grew concerned for Indigo and Carlos. Despite their crimes against me, I didn't want them to get hurt.

Arak was becoming more and more agitated. I sent soothing thoughts his way. He calmed down a bit and settled on the ground next to me. He was silent in my mind, though, simply radiating concern for Indigo. I was edging towards the tunnel when Arak startled and leaped shrieking into the air. Seconds later a loud explosion sounded from the tunnel. Dust and smoke whooshed out of the entrance in a wide arc. The tunnel had collapsed.

14 RESCUED BY CARLOS AND INDIGO (AGAIN!)

I threw down my mind's protective wall and Indigo came flooding in. But impressions of him came in a mix of jumbled thoughts, and I couldn't make out anything coherent. I cried his name out involuntarily.

- Indigo! -

Carlos stumbled out of the tunnel, dragging a limp Indigo, and closely followed by Churros. All three were covered in dust and debris and Indigo's forehead was covered in blood. The gnomes and Orlando were nowhere to be seen.

"Carlos!" The relief that poured into me as both Carlos and Indigo come out of the tunnel made a mockery of my commitment to harden my heart towards them.

"Jasmine. We must go quickly. Orlando is trapped behind the tunnel collapse for now, thanks to the gnomes, but that won't hold him for long and we need to regroup before meeting him again."

"Is Indigo alright?"

"Yes, I think so. But he shouldn't have gone in. The underground is no place for an Air Guardian. Pachamama knows what drove him to do it."

I looked down guiltily. I had. I tried and failed to stand up. Carlos looked at me and back at Indigo slumped against him.

"We need help." He looked around as if help might suddenly appear. "We have already asked so much of this place … there will be consequences."

We heard a car approaching fast. It screeched to a halt at the end of the dirt track near the tunnel entrance. I recognised it as Cherie's mum's Holden just as the driver's door was flung open and Cherie yelled, "Get in!"

"I asked you to stay on the main road," Carlos glared at her.

Cherie rolled her eyes at him. Mine teared up with affection and sheer pleasure at seeing her again, alive and … well ... so Cherie.

Carlos hauled Indigo into the back seat, then came and lifted me and my griffin easily from the ground. He looked down at me and held me tighter than he needed to. I wanted to throw my arms around his broad chest and bask in the comfort and bliss that would bring, but I resisted, even when he whispered quietly into my ear as he strode to the car.

"I thought I'd lost you, cara mia."

I didn't know Spanish, but that sounded like an endearment. Bastard, I thought, and stiffened. Playing games even now, trying to make me think he cared for me. He sensed the change in me as he released me gently onto the backseat next to Indigo. I winced in pain as I bent my wounded leg to fit.

"Come on, come on. You can have lovey-dovey cuddles later. Let's go before that Orlando guy shows up!" Cherie yelled.

Carlos slammed the door and whistled. Churros leaped at Carlos as if he were about to attack. The wolf shrunk as he flew, and a white glow surrounded him. A second later, Carlos held up a hand and caught his soul stone before it hit him. He got into the car as Cherie engaged first gear and planted her foot. I tried not to grimace, cradling my little griffin carefully, as we bunny-hopped over the dirt road until Cherie managed to sort it out. She'd had a few lessons with my dad but was by no means a good driver and didn't even have a learner's licence yet.

Indigo lolled next to me until his head fell onto my lap. I lifted the griffin out of the way and cradled Indigo's injured head - he was bleeding from a nasty looking gash just above the hairline. He was quiet in my mind, but I knew he was alright because I could sense him there.

"What just happened to your dog? Where did it go?" Cherie asked with a wild look.

"Just roll with it, Cherie," I suggested. "It's only going to get weirder; I promise you."

Out the window was the comforting sight of Arak winging along beside us, easily keeping up despite our speed.

"And what happened to you, Jas? You're a mess. You all are. Honestly, I leave you alone for two minutes, and you get attacked by a bear, taken advantage of by overly good-looking foreigners..." (glares here for Carlos and Indigo) "drugged and kidnapped by *the* creepiest looking dude I have ever seen! And I think you also went to a soccer training camp somehow, but I can't be sure about that. You hate team sports!"

I didn't even know where to begin. Carlos was giving me a meaningful look and I suspected he wanted me to keep quiet about ... well, everything. This only made me determined to tell her the whole story. We had reached the main road, though, and Carlos wanted Cherie to pull over so he could drive.

"What? No! I can drive just fine. Anyway, this is my mum's car, and I can't let anyone else drive it. She'd kill me."

"She might kill you anyway, Cherie. She never lets you borrow it, does she?" I couldn't help saying.

Carlos tried again. "Cherie, you are not a particularly safe driver. Please pull over and let me drive."

"Sure, I will. If you tell me everything that's going on."
Cherie swerved too fast around a sharp corner.

We all winced and Indigo groaned.

"Just tell her, Carlos," I piped up. "It'll be easier and
safer for everyone. If you don't, I will anyway."

Carlos frowned, but Cherie had already pulled over, so
he wasted no time in swapping places. The exchange took
barely a moment, and we were underway much more
smoothly, although Carlos muttered something about
horrible polluting petrol cars.

He offered Cherie no explanations though. He just
drove and stared straight ahead as we left the country lane
and turned onto the island's main ridge-top road. Cherie
turned to me expectantly and her mouth formed a wide O
of shock as she took in the griffin.

"What *is* that Jas?"

"My Spirit Companion. She's a griffin. She came to me
after I went into a spirit-awakening trance while I was in
Orlando's clutches." 'Clutches' sounded a bit dramatic, but
it fit. There was a lot of drama going on in my life.

Carlos caught my eye in the rear-view mirror. "Let your
companion petrify, Jasmine. It is the only way to restore
her."

"How do I do that? Oh, you mean let her turn back into
stone?"

I looked down at the griffin and before I could even
wonder how to achieve it, she shrank and glowed the way
Churros had, until I held a warm, dull stone in my hand. I
carefully put the stone in my pocket, ignoring Cherie's
incredulous look.

"To cut a very long story short, these guys ..." I indicated
Indigo and Carlos, "have informed me that I'm a
descendant of an ancient godlike race with magic powers
called the Guardians. They've come here to woo me in a
ridiculous competition. The first to make me fall in love
with them becomes the most powerful Guardian ever, and

then they can go destroy humanity or save it, or whatever they want to do."

"Jasmine, no!" Carlos protested.

"Petal. It's not like that." Indigo sat bolt upright. Clearly, he'd been shamming semi-consciousness for who knows how long, while I had been absent-mindedly stroking his hair.

"Whatever," I said, and carried on. "Orlando is some sort of mega-villain who wants me to team up with him to achieve his own agenda, whatever that is. While he held me captive, he told me a few useful things amongst his creepy lies. I spent half the time in my spirit-awakening trance though. Which was … amazing."

Cherie stared intently at the road. I knew she'd been listening, but it was a lot to process, and she didn't say anything for a minute or so, until: "Right. Well, that was illuminating. Not! I can see that there are super-strange things happening around you or because of you. I'm not sure if you can trust these guys or not. They're way too charming and good-looking to be completely real. And what a story: they both came here to woo you! Not that you aren't woo-worthy, babe, you just don't seem to realise it… but this is all totally crazy."

I was sure it did sound totally crazy.

"Jasmine," Carlos said earnestly. "Things are not always as they seem. I know you have every right to distrust us and our intentions."

"Stop, Carlos!" I interrupted angrily. "I don't want to hear it, okay, and I have no intention of helping you with this stupid challenge! Just tell me what happened after Orlando took me. Are Josh and Tina alright? How did you finally find me? And why didn't you find me sooner? I was in the exact spot you were going to check out when you rode off and left me with Indigo."

"Tina's fine," Cherie said quickly. "Josh is not so good, though. He tried to stop Orlando. We both did, but he threw us aside as if we were dolls. Josh hit the wall and I landed on him. He saved me from injury, but he's in hospital with concussion. They think he'll be alright, but he's been in and out of consciousness."

My heart fell right through my toes. I had to disentangle my friends from this right now.

"Carlos, take a right here and then a sharp left."

Carlos looked at me and nodded slightly as he followed my directions. Cherie didn't notice we were now on track to her house.

She carried on. "Carlos showed up not long after the ambulance left with Josh and I didn't let either him or *that* one," she nodded at Indigo, "out of my sight. I knew eventually they'd lead me to you, even if I did have to put up with them bickering like two old men the whole time. We've been combing the island for days looking for you without any luck, until suddenly about an hour ago they both stopped dead in their tracks and said they knew exactly where you were."

That must have been the moment I finally connected with the Earth in the tunnel and called for help, reaching Indigo through the Wind's Kiss and Carlos through our shared Earth Guardian connection.

"I count myself a fool for not realising where you were Jasmine, but Orlando laid us several false trails," Carlos apologised.

"Jasmine," Indigo said quietly. "I owe you a thousand and one apologies for letting Orlando take you. It was all my fault. I ... well ... I really wanted you to have a good time after all you'd been through. I wanted to see you happy again, like you were in the garden."

Carlos grunted and gripped the wheel tighter. No doubt he had already had words with Indigo because he restrained himself now. It was the kind of thing Carlos would never have done, I suspected – take risks for fun. I was even angrier, though, remembering Indigo's kiss at the restaurant. True, I'd had an amazing time, but Orlando had destroyed any pleasant memories when he helped me to see Indigo and Carlos's manipulation for what it was.

I ignored Indigo and spoke to Cherie again, "What about Mum and Dad? Haven't they been looking for me too?"

"Well … for some strange reason they also seem to think you've gone on a soccer training camp on the mainland. Once minute they were ringing constantly, asking if I'd found you yet, and then the next, they told me you were perfectly alright and had been on a camp for two days. When everyone knows you hate team sports! In fact, everyone seems to think this now except for Tina and Koro."

"And Duncan?"

"Oh yeah. Duncan. He totally knows something is up, especially with your parent's strange behaviour. He knows everything is connected: Josh's injury, your disappearance, the attacks by the leshy and sleazy Chad. But no-one else will listen to him and we've been trying to stay clear of him really."

Carlos pulled up outside Cherie's house, sparing me from trying to explain how Orlando had caused everyone's perceptions of reality to go wonky, except Tina and Josh's family apparently.

Cherie woke up to where we were.

"What are we doing here? I don't think we should drop the car off yet. We still need it."

Nobody said anything and Carlos and Indigo both seemed to be waiting for me to take the lead.

"Cherie …"

Understanding dawned on her face. "Oh, no you don't, sister! I'm not getting out here. Look what happened last time I left you. No way. Uh-uh, I ain't budging."

"Cherie. You know that Jasmine is involved in something very dangerous and frankly quite beyond your understanding." Carlos began.

"Oh, come on, dude," said Cherie. "I've been pulling my weight the past couple of days. You guys would've been at each other's throats the whole time instead of looking for Jas if I hadn't been here to bang your heads together."

Both guys looked a bit ashamed.

"It's true we would have wasted some time without you Cherie" Indigo responded. "Your knowledge of the island has been very useful. But this is for the best. You really don't know what you're up against and we can't afford to be looking after you *and* Jasmine at the same time."

This cast Cherie and me in the 'damsel in distress' role, and I could see by the look on her face that she found this as irritating as I did. There was no way she'd agree to leave me now.

I tried anyway. "Cherie, I think you should just go home and be patient. Maybe it's best that people do think I'm on a soccer training camp." I put my hand on her arm and looked as earnest as I could, for all the good it would do. But I knew Cherie wouldn't abandon me when I needed her. She was just awesome like that.

I was wrong. Cherie smiled brightly and reached for the door handle. "Alright, Jas. Catch you later. Have fun at soccer camp." Then she looked around in confusion. "What are these guys doing here? Isn't he the guy from the vineyard?" She pointed at Carlos, and I saw with a sinking heart what I had just done.

I looked away from Cherie in shame, but I didn't try to stop her as she shrugged and got out of the car. I had manipulated her emotions and reinforced Orlando's own lie that I was fine, and away playing a stupid team sport. I was as bad as Carlos, Indigo and perhaps even Orlando. A few sad flowers grew down past my eyes and I dashed them away angrily.

Carlos gave me an understanding look and Indigo raised one eyebrow, but neither said anything.

I grabbed the door handle and got out on one leg, leaning against the car to remain upright. Now I understood how easy it was to give in to temptation. I had to forgive Indigo and Carlos for manipulating my emotions or prove myself the worst kind of hypocrite. I'd gone further than they had, too and completely toyed with Cherie's reality not just made her feel less stressed or follow a suggestion. They both followed me out of the car and Carlos pressed the keys into Cherie's hand.

"My thanks to you and your mother for the use of the car Cherie ... and everything else."

She smiled at him hesitantly and started up the path to her house.

I bit my lip to keep from crying at how I had just treated Cherie. I started to limp up the path after her, hoping I could reverse what I'd done.

Carlos grabbed my arm. "You have no other way to protect her, amiga. You know that you have only done this for her."

Of course, he was right. Cherie would never leave me alone if she thought I needed her, and I did need her. But I had to let her go or she would end up hurt, or worse. In my shame and frustration, I lashed out at Carlos and Indigo.

"I wish you'd all just go away! You and your evil buddy and your stupid challenge!"

I lurched away from them ... and of course stumbled and fell as my injured leg gave way. I yelled in pain as I landed heavily on the hip pocket I had put Harriet, in soul stone form, in. Carlos gently pulled me up and swept me into his arms (yes, again) as he strode away from Cherie's house. I sighed with angry embarrassment, only glad that nobody was out on the street to witness this. Except for the birds, bees and wildflowers alongside the path, which all seemed to be smiling in approval at me and Carlos. Stupid flowers.

"I hear you, Jasmine, and you have my word that as soon as we have defeated Orlando and you are safe, I promise I will leave – if that is what you want."

"Wow, um okay." That took the wind out of my sails. I looked expectantly at Indigo as he loped along next to us, still looking pale and out of sorts.

"Yeah, what he said," he muttered.

"But won't you get in trouble with your councils, your

parents – and, well, um – your gods?"

Before either could answer, Carlos and Indigo stopped suddenly, and Indigo whispered, "Stay still, very still!"

Carlos was already still, but I squirmed around to see what the problem was. He clasped me tighter to stop me.

"What is it?" I whispered, trying not to panic.

But I didn't need their answer. I saw what they'd seen. There was a colourful shimmer in the air about a hundred metres up the hill ahead of us. Like a heat haze, if a heat haze could be bright orange.

"I can sense its affinity with the air," Indigo whispered. "It must be a powerful air creature. Sometimes if you are very still such spirits cannot sense or see you."

He was wrong about this. The orange shimmer was growing more substantial, turning into flames, then into a giant flame-coloured bird. For a moment I appreciated its beauty, before it fixed its orange eyes on us and, with a piercing, angry shriek, hurtled straight at us.

15 RECOVERY

"Heavenly Sky Father, it's the Vermillion Bird!" exclaimed Indigo "What is it doing here? It never leaves China! Take her and go, Carlos. I've got this."

"You can't defeat the Vermillion Bird alone. It's an elemental creature!" Carlos argued.

"I don't need to defeat it and I wouldn't want to hurt it anyway. I can handle it!"

Indigo raised his arms and summoned a horizontal tornado, which whirled out and embraced the fiery bird, halting it just before it struck us. Indigo's face was tight with concentration, and his long blond hair whipped about his face in the wind he had created. Arak hovered above his shoulder, screaming defiantly. With all the racket from the wind and the birds, it was surprising the whole street hadn't come out to see what was going on. A few dogs were barking madly, but no people appeared.

"Look, I've totally got this, Carlos. Just go!"

Carlos stood frozen with indecision as Indigo, who had not been in good shape to begin with, started to tremble visibly as the fire-bird fought to escape the tornado.

"Ach, for goodness sake!" I squirmed and pushed until Carlos was forced to put me down. I leaned on his shoulder.

"Show me what you need," I demanded as I opened my mind to Indigo. He hesitated a moment before responding.

- Just keep your mind open to me and feel the wind on your face, Petal -

There was a lot of wind coming off Indigo's tornado. It was not hard to focus on the feeling of it buffeting my face and body. Immediately, air started to pour into me, whistling with an ecstatic voice in the deepest corners of my mind and filling me with a sense of wild strength and invulnerability. Gratitude washed over me from Indigo as this strength flowed though me and into him. His tornado grew larger and wilder, eclipsing the fiery bird and almost drowning out its cries. Indigo made a final grand flourish with his hands and the tornado and it's occupant flew high above us and out over the ocean.

"What a rush!" I cried out as the wind departed, leaving me hollowed out, small and vulnerable again.

Indigo turned to me, the blood on his forehead dramatic against his pale face.

"Thanks, Petal, you were brilliant. I knew there had to be advantages to the Wind's Kiss! Now let's get going before something else happens," Indigo said before he collapsed in a heap in front of us.

Arak shrank into a soul stone and fell on top of Indigo's body. I wanted to collapse as well. Whatever I'd just done with Indigo had cost me the last shreds of energy after the recent ordeals. I clung to Carlos as my sight blurred and patted him gently on the shoulder.

"It's all on you Carlos dude. Whizz up your magic horse or whatever and get us out of here."

"There will be consequences ..."

I didn't hear him finish this sentence as I passed out.

*****

I awoke in Carlos's cottage in the sweet room I had taken a shower in before. Soft moonlight flooded the room through the open curtains. I noticed sadly that the bed cover was no longer pristine. It was wearing all the dirt and blood from my recent experiences. My leg and head no longer hurt. I carefully put my foot on the floor and went to stand up. It worked as good as new. I could get used to this benefit of magic. Of course, I wouldn't need all this magical healing without the constant onslaught of injuries that came with the magic.

I looked around for signs of Carlos or Indigo and saw Churros asleep on the floor. He woke as I made a move for the bathroom, and jumped on me, licking my face and knocking me back onto the bed.

"Wow, Churros, woah! It's super good to see you too."

Churros subsided and leant against me, pinning me to the bed.

My soul stone was lying on the bedside table and I reached for it. It came to life dramatically, flaring brightly before transforming into my little griffin. I heaved a sigh of relief as she leaped into the air with a joyful call, circling the room before settling down next to me and snuggling up with a contented purr. She had recovered from her injuries too. I laughed in delight.

Carlos appeared in the doorway, summoned by our ruckus. He looked exhausted with but was immaculate in dark blue jeans and white linen shirt.

"Carlos, how did we end up back here?"

"By magic horse, of course." He smiled at me.

"A taxi would have worked too, wouldn't it?"

"We didn't have time to wait for one and, given your recent experiences, it was as likely to be a leshy that showed up as a human driver."

"Too true." I looked around. "Where's Indigo?"

The humour left Carlos' voice. "The Sky Guardian was not as easily healed as you. He was injured worse than he would admit fighting Orlando, and then pushed himself too far to vanquish the Vermillion Bird. I had to ask for help from the forest spirits to restore Indigo. He is outside in the giant tree you can see from the doorway. I think it is called a cow-rie. It is a very wise old tree and was very welcoming when I first arrived here."

I couldn't help smiling at Carlo's pronunciation, even as I wondered how on Earth it would help Indigo to be up a kauri tree.

"But he'll be okay, won't he?" I could hear the concern in my own voice, so I deflected. "And what was that burning bird thing?"

Despite everything, I did care about Indigo. Carlos looked away with an unreadable expression on his face.

"The bird is a very strong elemental creature almost never seen outside of Asia and is usually very shy and peaceful. Pachamama only knows how Orlando managed to get it here. And yes, I think Indigo will recover fully, but he will not be with us for several more hours."

He took a deep breath and his tone changed.

"Jasmine, I am so sorry that you have experienced this awful time in your own community. If I had known such a thing would happen, I never would have come here and brought this trouble to you."

I wasn't ready to forgive Carlos or Indigo for their deceit, but I couldn't really regret that they'd come into my life. Even if they left me with a broken heart, they had brought so much colour, excitement, and magic.

"Carlos, maybe Orlando would never have come here if you and Indigo hadn't led him here, but … well, without you, I might never have found out who I am."

"And who might that be?" Carlos looked at me.

"Well, I guess I'm just me, but I'm a Guardian as well now, and I'm grateful for that." The spirit-awakening trance had given me confidence and I no longer felt so lost and overwhelmed by the incredible changes in my life.

"I am glad to hear you say that Jasmine. I have not enjoyed watching your confusion and doubt." Carlos smiled warmly at me. "Usually, there is a big celebration when a Guardian awakens to the Earth Mother. I wish you could have had such a celebration instead of this … this chaos."

He became all business again. "I am also sorry I couldn't completely heal you, either. I could only manage your leg injury before I needed to rest. May I help you with that now?"

I nodded and Carlos sat next to me on the bed, placing his hands on my shoulders. He slowly stroked his hands down my arms to my fingertips and back up again.

"How long have I been … asleep?" I needed distraction from his nearness and touch.

"It is nearly dawn now, so about sixteen hours, I think," he answered as he soothed away all aches and pains with his wonderful hands.

"When you channel a lot of the Sky or Earth's energy your body needs a lot of rest to recover, and you were already exhausted and injured during your escape from Orlando. There are consequences for using your power."

"You keep talking about consequences, but how can using the Sky and Earth's energy cause problems?"

"The more energy you channel, be it from the Earth or the Sky, the more it will take from your own life energy. A Guardian's power is directly related to the amount of life energy they are gifted with at birth. The exception is when you ask the creatures of Earth and Sky to help you. Then you aren't using your own life energy, but theirs. There is still a price to pay for that."

"That sort of makes sense, I suppose. Umm …". I caught a whiff of myself as I bent to inspect Carlos' work in healing my bruises. "I would really *love* a shower … that is, if we're safe now?"

Nothing had tried to attack or kidnap me the whole time I had been asleep. This seemed like a remarkable reprieve, given Orlando's track record of relentless attacks.

"The Sky Guardian and I spent some time creating powerful defences around this house so that we could bring you somewhere safe when we found you. This also has asked a lot of the island, but it was worth it. Help yourself, Jasmine, and I will fix you something to eat." He noticed he was still stroking my arms absently and stopped.

I practically skipped into the shower to remove the dirt from my ordeal with Orlando. Again, the shower was bliss. It had been. Way. Too. Long. I helped myself to the clothes in the cupboard. Unfortunately, there were only dresses left now, so I chose a simple white and blue striped dress that fell just past my knees and swirled in a satisfying fashion. I never wore dresses, but this one was very comfortable and made me review my prejudices. I combed out my wet hair and fixed it into a tight braid. Sighing with satisfaction, I headed out to the living room accompanied by my little griffin.

Carlos stared at me longer than was polite as I entered the living room in the soft dawn light. I probably looked silly in the dress. The sun was peeking above the ocean and lit the scene outside the windows; the view was much more stare-worthy than me. I stared back at Carlos till he dropped his gaze and apologised.

"I am sorry, chica, you look so, um …. nice … in a dress." Nice, huh. Sure.

I sat at the kitchen table and got straight into the warm porridge with mushed apple that Carlos laid in front of me. I'd missed way too many meals lately.

"Where did all these clothes come from, anyway?" I asked when I came up for breath.

"My mother found this place and furnished it with everything she thought I might need. And everything she thought you might need, just in case."

"Seriously?" All this implied that somebody had known about me before I knew anything about them. It was hard to imagine Carlos having a mother at all; he seemed so self-contained and independent. She was obviously a woman of good taste (even though it was not my taste) with plenty of money.

"I am glad to see your Spirit Companion is fully recovered." Carlos quickly changed the subject.

"Mmmm. Harriet is in great spirits now." I smiled at my

little griffin.

"Harriet? An interesting name."

"Was there a list I'm supposed to pick from?"

Carlos looked at me as if not sure what to make of this, and then he laughed. I hadn't heard him laugh before. I wished he'd do it more often because it suited him.

"Some Earth Guardians are a bit caught up in tradition and keep reusing the same Spirit Companion names, but of course Churros is not one of these." He smiled at this. Churros seemed an unlikely Guardian name and it spoke volumes about Carlos that he'd named his wolfish soul after a sweet, puffy confectionery.

"Well, Harriet it is then. Can I borrow your phone to call Tina and see how Josh is doing?"

"Yes, of course. I was about to do this myself, but no doubt you would prefer to."

As Carlos put his phone in my hand, I missed my own phone, lost at the bottom of the ocean. It's hard for a teenage girl to go as long as I had without checking my socials, liking my friends' posts, and taking selfies. Well okay, I wasn't a selfie-taking kind of teen, but even I was not above the addictive call of a smart phone (no pun intended).

"Um… I don't know Tina's number. It was stored in my phone under her name" I bit my lip in frustration.

"I know you won't like this Jasmine and I apologise now for the invasion of your privacy, but I have all your friends' numbers in my phone, if you look."

Carlos looked ashamed as he said this. I flipped through his address book and I saw he was not exaggerating. He had Cherie, Tina, Josh and my parents' numbers all filed neatly with first and last names. And what! My school principal's details?

"Right. I see." Only really, I didn't. It was too intrusive, like the clothes in the wardrobe in my size. There were a lot of strangers out there who had an agenda for me. Suppressing the anxiety this gave me, I selected Tina's name and called her.

"Jasmine!" Tina's achingly familiar voice leapt out of the phone. "Where are you? Who are you with? Are you okay?"

I thought carefully and decided avoidance was the best strategy. I didn't want to make the same mistake that I had with Cherie and then manipulate Tina's emotions and thoughts after I'd told her too much.

"Oh, I'm fine," I replied breezily. "How's Josh doing?"

"Josh is … well we think he's going to be okay. He finally woke up this morning and the first thing he did was ask after you. But I didn't know what to tell him. What's going on – where have you been? I called Cherie last night and she said you were at a soccer training camp or something ridiculous. Then her mum called me all freaked out, saying that two men had been there and taken Cherie away!"

"What? Did she say what they looked like?"

"No, she didn't say anything else. Jasmine, I'm afraid. What's happening? Is Cherie alright?"

Oh crap, crap, crap! Orlando hadn't been able get to me, thanks to Carlos and Indigo's protection, so he'd gone after Cherie. He was never going to give up and leave me alone.

"Tina … I … um, I'll sort it out. I'll get Cherie back, don't worry. Just look after yourself and Josh."

I hung up before she asked any more questions. I sat for a moment in stunned silence, immobilised by the thought of Cherie in Orlando's hands. Harriet laid a paw on my arm at my distress.

"What is it, Jasmine? What has happened?" Carlos asked me from across the table.

"Orlando has Cherie, Carlos. I thought I was protecting her by lying to her and leaving her alone, but I just made her vulnerable. We must get her back. Now!" I scooped Harriet up in my arms and rushed to the door.

"Wait, Jasmine…" Carlos began, but was stopped by a knock at the door just as I put my hand on the knob.

I flung the door open recklessly to see what new problem I could add to my list. Standing on the doorstep was the last person I wanted to see.

16 I AM FORCED TO FINISH THE STUPID CHALLENGE

Chad looked even more dishevelled and feral than the last time I had seen him. His clothes looked slept-in and his eyes were hollow, looking past me to some distant point. He raised a shaky hand towards me.

"I … you. Aaagh," Chad was struggling to speak. I snorted in disgust and started to close the door.

Carlos reached past me and held it open. "Jasmine, he has something to say."

As if Carlos' words had anchored him, Chad pulled himself up and a semblance of normalcy appeared in his eyes. He looked at me directly and his lips curved in a sneer. "Hey, babe. I've got a message for you from Orlando. He's got your home-girl and if you want to see her back the same way you remember her, you need to do what I say."

I bristled with anger and responded with a sneer of my own. Who uses 'home-girl'? What a loser this guy was. I wanted to throttle him when I remembered how he attacked me in the vines, but I needed to hear what he had to say. Cherie was the most important thing right now. Flowers started raining from my head as I struggled with my emotions. I shook my head to try and make it stop.

"Follow through with the challenge and tell the Earth Mother and Sky Father that you choose Orlando. Do not attempt to do anything else or choose anyone else. Orlando is watching you."

Carlos protested, "Pachamama

and the Padre de Cielo will see through such deceit. How does Orlando expect this to work?"

Chad sneered again, "That's her problem." He gestured at me. "She can figure it out. If she doesn't …" He shook his head with a mock sad expression.

Then, strangely, he stared off into the distance as he shifted from foot to foot. Then he grasped his head in his hands and started shrieking, "I can't … gah ... Get it out of my head! I'm sorry - it wasn't me."

"For crying out loud," I muttered and tried to shut the door on him.

Carlos intervened again. "He is suffering from Orlando's interference, Jasmine. We need to help him."

"Help him! He's a complete creep, Carlos, and besides we haven't got time!" I shouted.

Carlos looked at me. "You know we can't leave him like this, Cherie. He has been interfered with by Orlando and no one else can help him."

"Interfered with? I don't think you quite mean that, but I get what you're saying. See if you can fix him up, but he'll still be a creep." I wasn't in the mood to play nurse to Chad.

I remained leaning on the door with my arms folded as Carlos patiently lead the mumbling, shaking Chad to the kitchen table. Carlos sat face to face with Chad and put his hands on his temples. Chad instantly stilled and looked up at Carlos like a lost puppy. Jealousy and shame stirred in me. Jealousy at Chad receiving Carlos' full attention and shame that I had not realised that Chad was also a victim of Orlando. Churros came over and put his paw on Chad, licking his face.

"You too, Churros?" I muttered.

Churros glanced at me and whined.

Chad looked calm and relaxed beside Carlos, until he suddenly burst out crying.

"Oh, thank you, thank you, man. I can finally think again! He made me do … so many things." He turned to me. "It wasn't me; I swear it, it wasn't me. I wouldn't force a girl. You're not even my type!"

After this outburst, he carried on sobbing quietly while Carlos patted his back as if he did this sort of thing all the time. He probably did. He really was an upstanding guy for someone so young, especially when people needed help. So, the incident in the vines had not been all Chad's fault; I could chalk that one up to Orlando, too. Orlando, Orlando, Orlando. He had to be stopped because he was messing with my life.

Carlos led Chad into the living room and onto the sofa. Chad was still sniffling. Carlos smoothed Chad's brow and he relaxed and lay back, falling asleep as we watched.

"It will take a long time and he will need a lot of kindness and attention if he is to fully recover, but this is the best I can do for now," he said.

"That was amazing," I said, looking at Carlos with new respect.

He looked away, as if my words had embarrassed him.

I moved away brusquely, embarrassed as well.

"Right," I said purposefully. "Let's get Indigo out of the kauri tree, make a plan to get Cherie back, and get rid of Orlando before he screws up anybody else's life."

"Okay, Jasmine. Indigo won't be fully recovered yet, but you are right that all three of us need to decide what to do. You won't be able to successfully meet Orlando's demands: Pachamama and the Sky Father will read your heart whatever you tell them. They will see your truth."

I shrugged. I had no intention of meeting Orlando's demands. I doubted he would hold up his end of the bargain. I had something else in mind.

Giant sunflowers nodded their heads in the sunshine as

we headed into the garden, and I could hear a quiet murmur of voices. This garden felt like home now. It brought me a greater sense of welcome and peace than I had ever known. I looked up and caught Carlos looking at me with a warm smile.

"You are one of us, Jasmine – an Earth Guardian. This garden will always be your special place as it is where you first truly awakened to your power."

I wasn't sure I wanted to be part of Carlos' Guardian gang, to be honest, but I couldn't deny the power of the Earth and how wonderful it felt to use it. At the kauri tree, I instinctively placed my hands on its wide trunk and received the joyous welcome I was getting used to. I could sense the inner workings of the tree: the roots sucking up moisture from the ground and the leaves reaching out for sunlight and breathing in a reverse process to animals – out with the oxygen, in with the carbon dioxide. I looked deeper and 'saw' in the heart of the tree, in a hollowed-out space, an Indigo-like lump. He seemed to be part of the tree, and the cycling of nutrients, air and light was centred around him.

"Tree," I said. "I need him back now, please."

The tree hurried to oblige me, almost splitting itself in half to expel Indigo, naked and unconscious, from the base of its trunk. My immediate concern was for the tree, which looked horribly damaged by this process. I drew back in shock. Carlos stepped past me and laid his hands on the trunk. He muttered quietly and drew his hands up along the split, sealing it as he did so. By the time he had finished, the trunk looked like it had always had, with an Indigo-sized knot near its base. Carlos sat down heavily on the grass when he had finished.

He looked up at me. "I would perhaps have done what you did a bit more delicately, Jasmine. We must put back what we take from Pachamama. That is partly why using her energy takes energy from us."

"Oops, sorry. I'm really worried about Cherie – and

Indigo. I don't normally rush in like this."

"I know, Jasmine, it's alright. The Air Guardian can have this effect on people."

I stiffened. I didn't like to think of myself as vulnerable to Indigo's charms. Besides, I was more concerned with Cherie right now.

Carlos rose wearily to his feet and shuffled over to where Indigo lay. I turned away with my cheeks burning. At least he was on his stomach, with only his long lean back and taut buttocks on show. I clamped down on thoughts as they veered in the wrong direction, but it was too late, as Indigo's amused comment attested.

- Beware, Petal, I'm going to stand up now and you'll get to see *all* of me! -

I went and stood behind a giant sunflower, but inadvertently looked when Indigo yelped in pain. Again, I was blasted by Indigo's glory as he stood with Carlos' help and, grimacing, put his full weight on shaky legs. Indigo smirked at me. I turned and fled to the other side of the house.

"Tell me when he's decent, Carlos," I called as I left.

Harriet squawked as I accidentally yelled in her ear.

I found a quiet spot on the bank to sit half-shaded by tall grass and gazing on the water below. It grew too bright to look at, so I lay back and let myself relax despite my worries. The heartbeat of the Earth rose and engulfed me as it had in my mother's garden. I let it draw me in and distract me with its warm and comforting embrace.

Carlos' voice calling to me along the veins of the Earth drew me back to myself. Carlos knelt beside me and Indigo stood behind him, arms crossed and mercifully fully clothed. He was still pale and tired looking, but he had no visible injuries. A small part of the anxiety I'd been holding slipped away.

"I am sorry, Jasmine. Usually, we never interrupt another Earth Guardian in Pachamama's embrace, however, time is pressing," Carlos apologised as if he'd made a terrible social blunder, and I guessed for him that was so.

"I know, Carlos, it's fine, really. If you'd let me, I would have stayed there all day. What time is it?" The sun was high.

Carlos and Indigo exchanged a guilty look.

"It's past midday. Your communion with the Earth Mother seemed to be doing you a lot of good, Petal, so we didn't want to disturb you."

I smiled weakly. They were right. I didn't feel the same wild panic I had when Chad first gave me Orlando's message.

"We have been talking about the situation, Jasmine." Carlos looked at me cautiously, but my wee plug-in to the Earth Mother had chilled me out and I simply nodded for him to go on.

He drew a deep breath, then blurted, "The only path forward lies in completing the challenge. Once one of us receives Pachamama's and the Sky Father's gift, then we will be able to find your friend and defeat Orlando."

I was frowning, so Indigo leapt in: "Orlando will never hold to his word and give your friend back, Petal. Our history is littered with his lies and betrayals. And there is no way you can deceive the Sky Father and Earth Mother, telling them Orlando is your choice."

"Wow, that's your answer, guys? After you both promised you would abandon this stupid challenge if I asked you to!"

My chilled-out state was rapidly melting. Just when I'd started to trust them both, they proposed this. They did care more about winning the prize than anything else.

Carlos tried reasoning. "We cannot see any other way. I am sorry, Jasmine. Truly I am. We have not been able to defeat Orlando. Partly because he uses his powers unscrupulously and without care for their consequences, but he is also always two steps ahead of us and relentless in his assaults. We need more firepower, and this is the only way to get it."

"You're forgetting one small thing, dudes." I was seething now. They were back to manipulating me and trying to win the stupid challenge again, after all we'd been through and what they'd promised me.

"I am not *in love* with either of you." I should have found this conversation ridiculous and embarrassing, but anger and fear for Cherie helped me rise above my usual insecurities. "What will the Earth Mother and Sky Father do with that?" I challenged them triumphantly.

Then I did become embarrassed. Carlos said nothing and just looked at me. I could sense Indigo's amusement through our infernal mental bond as he looked me in the eye.

"Ummm. Do you really think that's true, Petal? The ancestors would not have picked us if they did not think we could form a connection with you."

If my face wasn't red before, it sure was now, and I couldn't prevent flowers streaming out of my head. A connection. What a way to put it.

"For crying out loud, Indigo, we had one kiss. You think you're so irresistible, but it didn't mean anything!"

I rushed on before either of them could reply, or I found out I was lying to myself. Even if the kiss had meant something, even if the thought of Indigo made my knees weak, and Carlos sent me spinning whenever he looked at me with his serious eyes, it didn't mean I was in love with either of them. It was just chemistry and physical attraction, right? Regardless, I was done being a pawn in other's games. There had to be a pathway that wasn't about meeting everyone's agenda but my own.

"No, I have another plan," I said. "I'll go and meet your ancestors or gods, or whatever they are, and tell them they need to save Cherie and get rid of Orlando. Once they see that I'm not *in love* with either of you they'll have to listen to me anyway. They'll have to find another way to choose between you."

Both Indigo and Carlos looked sceptical.

"I really don't know if that will work Jasmine," said Carlos. "It is true we often ask for Pachamama's help, and sometimes she even grants it, but it is always uncertain and often requires some sort of sacrifice."

"I hate to admit it, Petal, but this time the Earth Guardian is right. When you ask the Ancestors for help, it never turns out the way you expect. No-one fully understands what their motivations are and there is always a price to pay."

"I'll do whatever it takes to get Cherie back and get Orlando out of my life. If there is a cost, I will happily pay it. I don't have much to lose at this point."

"Well, they do say, Jasmine, that if your request is unselfish, it is more likely to be granted and with fewer consequences. I don't know if your request meets this criterion, but it may do." Carlos loved to talk about consequences.

"Don't give her false hope, man." Indigo glared at Carlos before turning to me. "You can't expect your plan to work, Petal. What happens when you go in front of the Earth Mother and Sky Father is completely unpredictable. And you can only get their attention if some strong emotion is driving you. I know this sounds corny, but only love will work for you. You're just not a hater."

I took a deep breath. "So be it then. I get that things are out of my control, and you and your buddies might just end up getting what you want, but I have to try it my way. I love Cherie, we've been best friends forever, so surely that will be enough. Now, how do we do this?"

Carlos and Indigo looked at each other, clearly exasperated by me or my naivety, or both. But then Indigo shrugged and made a go-ahead gesture to Carlos.

Carlos laid a hand on my arm, looking at me seriously. "You must go alone, to Uluru in Australia, a place where the Sky Father and the Earth Mother are locked in an eternal embrace. You must go during the solar eclipse marking one thousand years of the Guardians' split. This eclipse happens the day after tomorrow."

17 TO ULURU

"Australia! I don't even have a passport. How can I get there so soon? And what is Uluru even?"

"Uluru is a giant rock in the middle of the Australian desert. It's on all the Australian tourism posters. And don't worry about getting there," Indigo said confidently. "I can make a call and sort that out straight away."

Indigo stepped away to do just that, reaching someone in moments, speaking to them in a lyrical language that I didn't recognise. I chewed on my lip while he was gone and fiddled with the daisies in the grass. My touch turned them into giant versions of themselves, making it easy and satisfying to plait them into daisy chains. Carlos smiled at me and grew some beautiful flowers straight out of the ground, the perfect addition to my chains.

As we casually created small miracles, he said, "Jasmine, let me come with you. Orlando might try something else to make sure you do what he wants. We don't know what his end game is. This could all be some complicated ruse." Carlos was looking really worried, but for what or whom I could only guess.

"No," I said fiercely before my own fears and desires could change my mind. "Surely Orlando won't attack me if he thinks I'm doing what he wants. I need you both to stay here and protect my friends and family. I can't let anyone else I care about get hurt or taken. Josh and Cherie … it's too much. Promise me!"

"Carlos," Indigo stepped back into the conversation. "You know that Jasmine is badass. She is just as powerful as both of us combined, possibly more so. She can take care of herself."

I drew a shaky breath as Indigo championed me, not entirely sure he was right, but rolling with it anyway.

"She is untested and untrained. We cannot let her go alone!" Carlos exclaimed.

Indigo had the wall in his mind firmly up between us, but he was deliberately letting me feel his confidence in me.

"We owe her this, Carlos. We should have known Orlando would go after someone she cared about if he couldn't get to her. What would you want if you were her? You would want to protect your family at all costs, as would any clan member, Earth or Sky."

Calling on Carlos' obvious family values and protective instincts was the right way to get him to agree. He looked from Indigo to me with a sigh of resignation.

I nodded firmly. Yes, this is how I wanted it.

"Carlos, I also want you to remove any form of manipulation on my friends and family and heal them if they need it. I don't want any of them suffering the way Chad did. You'll have to tell them the whole truth about what's happened to me though."

Carlos argued half-heartedly about needing to keep my abilities and the challenge secret, but eventually agreed to make sure that my mum and dad, at least, knew everything.

The next few hours were a whirlwind of activity. Indigo sorted out my travel details and took a photo of me for the passport that his contact assured him would be waiting for us at the airport. There was no mention of money, so Indigo must have funded everything. The trip to Ayers Rock Airport, the closest to Uluru, would take at least ten hours and I had to leave first thing the next morning. I'd never travelled so far before and fretted about how I'd get from the airport to Uluru, but Indigo assured me he'd arrange for someone to pick me up, take me to a hotel for the night and on to Uluru the morning of the eclipse.

I knew that both Indigo and Carlos' people had considerable resources at their call, but the speed with which all this was organised spoke of some level of pre-planning. All the Guardians had a vested interest in getting me to Uluru in time. I just hoped that by going, I wasn't meeting everybody else's agenda except my own. I had no choices left to me now. Orlando had taken them away.

A little after midday, Carlos left to take Chad home. While Indigo was busy with my travel plans, Carlos had spent time with Chad, working his healing magic on him. I gave them plenty of space and stayed outside, letting the peace and comfort of the garden work on me, without losing myself in it as I had earlier. I accepted that Chad had not been to blame for everything that went on, but I didn't want to be near him.

Chad and Carlos left on foot, Churros trotting at their heels. Chad tried to talk to me as they left, but Carlos shook his head at him, and he left me alone. Carlos came back alone a couple of hours later with a bag packed full of my own clothes and other essential travel items. I sighed happily at the sight of my comfortable old clothes.

"How did you get all this Carlos – breaking and entering?"

"No-one was home, and your bedroom window was already broken so I let myself in. I didn't think you would mind. I can see that you are not so comfortable in the clothes that my mother chose, even though they do suit you."

"Yes … well, thanks, I guess."

"I have something else for you too, Jasmine. I know that you have been missing one."

He handed me a brand-new latest version smart phone

complete with a SIM card.

"OMG!" I shrieked, "you are the best!"

If the Earth Mother, or whoever, had been reading my heart just then, Carlos may well have been endowed with all the power in the world he could ever dream of.

Carlos looked overwhelmed by my response. "I, um, also loaded all the numbers onto it that you might need and some useful apps too. And don't worry about roaming charges in Australia as I've got you a good plan for that. There are also maps, music and a GPS tracker. Here, let me show you."

He flicked through the phone, pointing out all its highlights. He had put his phone number in, but not Indigo's. When I mentioned this, Indigo, who'd been watching from across the living room with a sour look, blew up a mini whirlwind and snatched the phone from Carlos. He quickly entered his number and handed it to me as I rolled my eyes at him.

Carlos coolly ignored the interruption. "You may want to call your parents, Jasmine. I am sure you want to hear their voices."

"Good idea."

Mum picked up on the first ring. "Hello. Jasmine is that you?"

"Mum! Yes, it's me."

"We've been so worried! For some reason, over the past few days we thought you were at a soccer training camp. But when we returned from the Frying Fish half an hour ago, we remembered everything ... how angry you were at me about your biological father, the bear and the ferry accident. What on earth's going on?"

Mum's voice had grown more frantic as she went on and then her voice abruptly took on the tone of parental authority. "Come home right now, Jasmine, do you hear me? Right now!"

"Mum, it's okay. Look I'm okay, but I can't come home yet. I promise I'll explain when I get back in a few days, but

I have to do something first."

"What could you possibly *have* to do, Jasmine? You're a seventeen-year-old high school student …"

I interrupted. "Mum, I've got to go. I'm not angry with you anymore. I understand why you didn't say anything about … you know … my biological father. I really do. And … I love you guys. Bye."

I hung up quickly before Mum could launch another tirade. The phone rang again straight away, but I ignored it. Carlos admitted he'd heard much of what my mother had said. She was almost yelling.

"I laid strong protections on your family's house while I was there. It must have broken Orlando's influence on your parents. It might mean he is no longer on the island if they were broken so easily."

"I'm glad," I replied fiercely. "I don't want Mum and Dad to be manipulated like that. It didn't help Cherie and it won't help them."

Carlos retired to the kitchen to whip up another delicious meal. Indigo took the opportunity, out in the garden, to show me a few helpful tricks if I was attacked. He also took every opportunity to get me in secluded corners away from Carlos's view. I wasn't interested in intimate moments with Indigo at that moment though and finally I'd had enough. Using one of his own tricks, I blew him away with a strong puff of air. Indigo went headfirst over the garden bench with a look of surprise. I couldn't help feeling satisfied with this result.

"You did say she was more powerful than both of us!" Carlos laughed and called out the kitchen window.

Surprisingly, Indigo laughed as well and declared the lessons over for the day.

As the day grew older, I grew more anxious. I'd never travelled overseas, which I know is surprising these days. To do so alone now, with all this heavy stuff going on was stressful. I was surprised I hadn't had another anxiety attack, but suspected that Harriet was protecting me from these. Any time I started getting agitated, she would come over and fluff around near me or peck my ear gently and I was instantly calmer. Churros and Harriet both snuggled up to me at the dinner table and Arak sat behind me. I was surrounded by protection and calm as I tucked into a strange curry concoction of mushrooms and a textured protein substance.

"This is delicious, Carlos, but what is it?"

"It's jackfruit. It's full of protein and other good stuff. All Earth Guardians are vegans. None of us can harm a living creature when we are so closely connected to them and feel their suffering and joys."

"Well, shouldn't that also go for plants then? I hear them talking to me all the time."

Carlos smiled as if I had something cute but silly. "I can see how you would think that, but all plant life is so connected to Pachamama that plants see themselves as one whole living entity. Everything can be renewed easily by Pachamama, so she is happy to give of herself as sustenance. It is only when entire forests and ecosystems are harmed that she suffers," Carlos explained.

This made a sort of sense to me and opened the evening to a long and interesting conversation on the harm humanity was wreaking on the planet, and by extension on the Earth Mother and the Sky Father. Indigo had a lot to say on the subject and it turned out that until he had been chosen for the prophets' challenge, he had been an intern at a start-up trying to suck carbon from the air. I didn't pretend to understand entirely how this could work, but I was very glad that he was clearly distancing himself from his people's militant approach to the world's problems.

Sometime later I found myself yawning and saw with surprise that it was midnight. I had enjoyed the evening and I hadn't noticed the time passing or thought too much about the next day. Even Carlos and Indigo seemed to be enjoying each other's company, laughing freely, and teasing each other good-naturedly about their opposing allegiances and opinions.

Excusing myself, I went to bed feeling relatively optimistic about what the morning would bring. Harriet nestled into my side and made soft cooing noises. As soon as I lay down, I fell asleep.

*****

I was woken from deep sleep by a knock on the door. Confused, I looked around in the pre-dawn light, unsure where I was or what was going on. It took a few minutes for everything to come back to me, and then anxiety gripped me and my stomach churned.

- Petal? Are you alright? You need to come now. The boat is ready, and we have to get you to the airport. -

- Coming - I replied automatically, no longer giving a thought to the strangeness of this communication. I pulled on my cargo pants and a Frying Fish shirt and did my teeth. My bag in hand, I headed outside to find Carlos and Indigo waiting for me.

"How are we getting to the airport?" I looked around and saw only Indigo's bike.

"I've organised a launch to get us to the city first. We don't want to risk taking public transport right now." Indigo took my bag and my hand as we headed down the garden, Carlos trailing behind. Just as at my own house, a private path led down to the beach. Indigo sensed my fear and hesitation at the reality of the day ahead.

- You've got this, Jasmine. I wouldn't let you go otherwise. -

This was somewhat reassuring, and the anxiety receded as my entourage of bird, wolf, griffin and hot heroes led me down through the bush to a pebbly bay below. Birdsong accompanied us in the early light and I heard a note of farewell in their music. I marvelled anew to hear such voices around me. I could lay some of my problems at the door of the Earth Mother right now, but I couldn't deny this gift she had given me.

At the bottom of the path, we found a sleek yellow

launch anchored just offshore. The small bay was otherwise empty as the boat purred quietly over to meet us.

"Electric, of course." Indigo grinned at me, and I rolled my eyes at his bragging.

Indigo looked smug as we entered the boat via a ramp. The pilot greeted Indigo as an old friend and didn't bat an eye at our furred and feathered companions, except to give my griffin an incredulous look. A seagull resting on his shoulder gave him away as an Air Guardian. I let myself feel a moment of bitterness that the Guardians, while not willing to help us with Orlando, were obviously keen to get me to Uluru.

I relaxed back into the luxurious seat and watched my island home recede. The memory of my near drowning played on my mind the whole trip, but surrounded by Harriet and everyone else, it didn't hold the terror it might have. That had been mere days ago, but it seemed like an age. We sped over the mirror-like water of the Hauraki Gulf into the steadily brightening day. I sighed and looked at my hands which were stroking Harriet, weighed down by the task in front of me. Carlos laid a hand lightly on mine, and Indigo let me know of his presence at the edge of my mind; a way more intimate touch than Carlos' physical one.

Just before we reached the city, we petrified our furred and feathered companions. As Harriet reverted to a stone, confidence left me. At the ferry terminal the pilot handed some keys and a large folder to Indigo and pointed towards the nearest parking building. Indigo led us into the carpark where we found an electric sportscar waiting for us. In the car he handed me the folder. I opened it to find a passport, an itinerary, and a pile of Australian cash. I didn't want to count it in front of Carlos and Indigo, but it was more cash than I'd ever held in my hands before.

Indigo drove us to the airport, weaving through Auckland's early morning commuter traffic without any difficulty. A wind was beginning to stir as we parked, and the trees in front of the airport were waving around as if bidding me farewell. It was a symptom of my strange new reality that I suspected they were doing exactly that.

Inside the terminal, Indigo headed off to check in for me. I only had a carry on bag, so Carlos walked me straight to the departure gates. We stopped at the entrance, and I shuffled awkwardly, trying to hide my fear at going on alone. Damsel in distress again: sigh.

Carlos looked at me with the intense gaze that always made me squirm and spoke to me for the first time since we'd left Waiheke. "Jasmine, mi corazón, I know you have difficulty believing in yourself and how amazing you are, but if you trust your heart, all will be well. I promise."

He reached towards me and I thought from his purposeful look that he was about to kiss me. This was his last chance to sway me to choose him, if it came to that, and he knew I'd shared a kiss with Indigo. I would have let Carlos kiss me then. I even longed for it. But he just hugged me fiercely, and for a long time we stood there, neither breaking away. My traitorous heart was fluttering as madly as if he was kissing me passionately. Our hearts synchronised and the sense of wellbeing, belonging and pleasure that we shared as two Earth Guardians connecting left me never wanting the moment to end.

We were both trembling slightly when he finally pulled away and stepped back. Without looking me in the eye he turned abruptly and left. I stared after him as people pushed past me into the departure lounge. Indigo strode towards me, and I wondered if he'd seen Carlos embrace me. Saying nothing, he stepped forward, looking at me for permission as he drew close enough for our foreheads to touch. I nodded slightly, knowing what he was about to do and knowing that I might not be ready for it. Indigo drew a shaky breath and I realised that he might not be ready for it either.

Then his forehead touched mine and Indigo shared *everything* he was feeling and thinking in that moment.

He had never intended to like me and had never wanted

to do as the prophets had asked. He hadn't wanted to manipulate an innocent girl's emotions and thought that the cost of being chosen to participate in the challenge would be too high. That was the reason his father had been in Auckland with him at first: to make sure Indigo didn't try to abandon the challenge. Which he would've done at the soonest opportunity, until he met me on the ferry and saw the flowers growing out of my head. I watched through his eyes as he first saw me sitting with my friends, looking so young and ordinary. I felt his initial disdain for me as I stumbled over and blushed, stammering out my request. Then I witnessed that disdain turn to something else when I smiled at him, and flowers blossomed in my hair – hope and a stirring of interest.

He saw me in Carlos' garden with Pachamama's life-force bursting out of me and everything blossoming dramatically, making me laugh in delight. All he wanted to do then was to stay in that moment forever. He hadn't felt true happiness as he did in that moment, for a long time. Not since his mother left – a little Indigo factoid I stored away for later. He cursed himself for how he behaved after we kissed at the restaurant. He had been shocked at the intensity of the kiss and had reacted in self-defence by pushing me away with his words. But he wanted me, just me, and he couldn't give a toss about the Earth Mother and Sky Father's prize. He never had.

Stunned by everything Indigo had shared, I stumbled away from him. I didn't open myself the way he had to me. Even in the face of his honesty, I just couldn't do it, and I didn't have a good reason. I was afraid of what I might reveal to *myself* and to him if I did, and how vulnerable that would leave me.

He just looked at me as I stepped back clutching my backpack tightly. Wordlessly, he handed me my passport and boarding pass. I fled through the boarding gate without looking back. Regret instantly filled me, and I turned, but he was gone. I let myself be pulled along by the crowd through customs and into the departure lounge.

I let go of any remaining doubt and anger at Indigo and Carlos then, though there was little left by now. They were just as innocent in all this as I was. I directed my anger towards Orlando, the rest of the Guardians and the Earth Mother and Sky Father who were all responsible for putting us in this ridiculous position.

Thoughts of Carlos and Indigo filled my mind after their poignant and loaded farewells, and I finally admitted to myself that I was deeply, madly head-over-heels for both of them. I was still determined to carry out my plan though. Whatever feelings Carlos and Indigo inspired in me, I would greet the Earth Mother and Sky Father on my own terms, and they would help me get Cherie back.

"First time travelling by yourself, Miss?" A voice shook me out of my thoughts, and I smiled automatically at the customs officer as I handed over my boarding card and passport.

The guard smiled back, and suddenly his features took a dramatic lurch and a leshy stared back at me.

"Don't forget," it hissed. "You mussst think only of Orlando when you speak to *them*. Or your friend will not come back to you."

I pulled myself up and silently stared it straight in the eye, without backing down. Then I stalked off to catch a plane alone and face down some gods and villains.

18 BETWEEN HEAVEN AND EARTH

So that's how I ended up walking around a big red rock in the middle of the Australian outback one summer morning. My feet hurt, the traumatic experiences of the past weeks were still with me, and I was afraid I wasn't going to make it before the eclipse at midmorning.

"Hsssssssssss."

I froze, sweat oozing down my forehead and into my eyes. I didn't want to turn around; I knew what I'd see. I moved faster, trying to outpace the leshy before it could reach me with its creepy eyes and unnatural strength. Then I heard Carlos's voice telling me to believe in myself, and Indigo reminding me that I was badass. Harriet, still in stone form in case we bumped into any tourists, vibrated in my pocket and I turned to face the leshy.

"Hssss. You mussst think only of Orlando when you speak to *them*!" it repeated what the leshy at the airport had said. Possibly it was the same leshy.

Darkness had been gathering with the impending eclipse. Gloom covered the rock and there were no tourists nearby. The further I got from the carpark, the more of them I'd left behind. Still, I had to be discrete. I called up a little windstorm as Indigo had shown me and thrust it towards the leshy. The leshy was gathered up with a pile of red dust and swept off into the desert, shrieking as it went: "Remember!"

I sent the windstorm miles away before releasing it into the desert and carried on with renewed speed. The leshy had reminded me of who I was and what I could do, so I started to use the air now to add speed to my steps, to make sure I got there in time.

And I did. Just before the eclipse reached its peak, I rounded a corner and saw what Carlos had described: a waterhole with the rock towering directly above it, and a gorge lined with the faint markings of ancient Aboriginal drawings leading into the folds of the rock itself. I paused at the waterhole, admiring the sight of crystal clear water in the middle of the hot, dry desert.

I walked as far as I could along the gorge and found an isolated crevice. I sat on the ground and waited the last few minutes for the sun to be completely eclipsed, unsure of what would happen next. I was surrounded by rock on three sides and the coolness of the crevice was welcome after the hot air and sun. I was finally deep within the heart of Uluru, as everyone seemed to want me to be, about to commune with the two most powerful beings in existence. To demand that they help me. No-one had told me what to do next, so I did the only thing I could and laid my hands on the bare rock, opening myself to the natural world as I'd learned to do in Carlos's garden.

I didn't let myself sink in the joyful welcome of the desert environment though. I focused on one thought: "Help me Earth Mother and Sky Father. Help my friend. Please." I tried as hard as I could not to even think of Orlando, Carlos or Indigo. No-one and nothing responded to my pleas, but in my heightened state of contact with the natural world I sensed two humans approaching down the path from the waterhole.

I opened my eyes, breaking off contact with the earth, to see Orlando and Cherie strolling down the gorge as if they were sightseeing. Orlando smiled when he saw me, like a cat who'd found some cream, but Cherie walked along with a vacant look. She was dishevelled, her clothes dirty and creased, a state she would hate.

"Cherie!" I shrieked and rushed from the crevice towards her.

Orlando raised a hand before I could reach them and held it towards me.

I found my feet firmly rooted in the rock. Cherie ignored me, her stare unbroken by as much as a blink.

"What have you done to her?" I yelled at Orlando, my voice echoing off the walls of the gorge. I struggled to free myself, too unnerved to think of calling upon the earth to help me.

"Jasmine, Jasmine. So much untrained power … You could easily release yourself if you wanted to."

"Why are you even here? I'm doing what you want!"

"Ah, Jasmine, that will never work. These are gods we're talking about. You can't deceive them and it's clear I am not your one true love." He leered at me.

At my confused look, he smiled calmly. "No, Jasmine, after you so rudely declined the invitation to join me, I knew you were unlikely to complete the challenge. You're too contrary to do the bidding of those foolish Guardians. But you do need to be here, my dear, and so I gave you incentive to come."

I was really confused now. What did this guy want?

"Come," he said. "Talk to the Ancestors and ask them for help to defeat me as you intend to do."

Before I could do anything else, he walked straight through the cave walls and into the rock itself, towing Cherie after him.

"Cherie – no!" My mind roiled as I rushed at the rock and pounded on it. Something heard me, and the red rock opened for me as well. I stepped forward and found myself falling through silent darkness, too petrified to scream.

Thousands of twinkling lights appeared to illuminate the

darkness. I slowed, falling more gradually, until I was floating, cradled in a gently sparkling, incredibly soft and cosy space. There was a tremendous sense of welcome, just like when I connected with the earth, but amplified a thousand times, and I was no longer afraid. In fact, I was so warm and comfortable, I wanted to stay where I was forever and forget all my problems. A voice spoke in my mind and reverberated throughout my body. It was male and female at the same time and felt immensely old.

DAUGHTER. YOU ARE WELCOME HERE.

I wondered where 'here' was, and my question was answered straight away.

YOU ARE IN OUR EMBRACE, DAUGHTER. YOU ARE BETWEEN THE HEAVEN AND THE EARTH.

So, I was speaking with the Earth Mother and Sky Father. I urgently formed my request to help Cherie and defeat Orlando before I could get lost in their embrace and forget myself and why I'd come, which seemed a real possibility.

YOUR FRIEND IS SAFE FOR NOW.

An image formed in the starry darkness of Cherie wandering through the bright green sage bushes of the outback. Then they showed me Orlando trapped in a red rock cavern, raging as he flailed his fists, demanding the earth obey him, to no avail.

YOUR FRIEND IS SAFE. OUR SON IS WITH US, BUT WE WILL NOT HOLD HIM FOR LONG AS IT IS NOT OUR PLACE TO DO SO.

I sighed and let go of my worry for Cherie. Wherever she was, it wasn't with Orlando. Maybe I should just let go of all my worries and fears and lose myself in the warm and welcoming embrace of the Ancestors. My problems were drifting away, including the Guardians and their agenda. Thinking about the Guardians reminded me of my anger at the Earth Mother and Sky Father for creating their ridiculous challenge that played with peoples' emotions and feelings. I remembered the feelings that Indigo and Carlos had stirred in me, whether I wanted them or not, and I confronted the gods with my anger.

They didn't apologise. They were elemental beings who lived only when they felt true passion and they could never apologise for stirring that in someone else.

HOLD ONTO YOUR PASSION AND ANGER, DAUGHTER. THAT IS WHAT ENABLES US TO COMMUNICATE RIGHT NOW. IT IS ALSO PART OF WHO YOU ARE AND IT PREVENTS YOU FROM LOSING YOURSELF HERE FOREVER.

They reached out and cradled me so close I could feel the shape of their hands around me. I was overwhelmed by warmth and love, by vast airy spaces and infinite possibilities all at the same time. For a moment or for a century, I could see and hear nothing but their eternal love for each other and for all life on earth.

I saw what a fool I had been. My plan had been plain silly. Trying to bend the will of these beings was like trying to push water uphill or change the colour of the sky. Just as Carlos and Indigo had said, they read what was in my heart as easily as if it were a picture book.

BECAUSE OF YOUR OPEN HEART AND GREAT CAPACITY TO LOVE, IT IS YOUR TASK TO UNITE OUR SUNDERED FAMILY AND HEAL THE EARTH.

"What do you mean? You want me to do what?" I found myself shouting into the void. More quietly I found myself asking, "Who should I choose?"

All I had in reply was a warm laugh and an unhelpfully vague response.

LISTEN TO YOUR HEART, DAUGHTER. IT KNOWS THE TRUTH AND IT WILL GUIDE YOU IN ALL THINGS.

"Wait!" I cried as their attention left me.

But I was ejected from their warm embrace and spat out into the wild and empty desert. The loss of the Sky Father and Earth Mother's embrace hurt me more keenly than anything ever had in my life. I fell to my knees and howled with loss and longing until I was wrung out with exhaustion and had no tears left to cry. I lay on the ground and let the steady heartbeat of the desert wrap me in comfort. It wasn't the same as being in the Sky Father and Earth Mother's embrace, but it helped a lot and eventually I felt strong enough to face reality again.

I sat up and saw that the solar eclipse was over. I couldn't see Uluru, or any sign of civilization and it was nearly dusk. Something glittered on the ground nearby. I was surrounded by hundreds of tiny diamond-like stones. One was stuck to my face, just under my eye, and I freaked out when I realised that the stones were my tears. My skin felt tight and had taken on a shifting brown-red hue. It was the colour of the ground at my feet and of Uluru. Under my skin, orange and blue swirled, like fire and water twining together. I felt my head, worried about what might have happened to my hair, and found only vines, leaves and flowers.

"Jas! Jasmine is that you?"

I leapt up as a figure came stumbling into view over a rise, my own troubles forgotten at the welcome sound of Cherie's voice.

"Cherie!" I cried out as she came near, and I rushed to embrace her.

We fell into each other's arms, and I buried my face in her shoulder. I could have stayed like that for ages, joy coursing through me at the return of my friend. But Cherie stiffened and stepped back from me abruptly. I took in the sight of her, alive and whole, if somewhat dishevelled. Her clothes and skin were covered with a fine layer of red dust. I smiled and stepped towards her again, but she looked afraid and uncertain and drew further away, rubbing her arms as she did so.

"Jasmine, is that really you? You don't look right, and you just zapped me with some weird kind of electric shock."

"Cherie, it's me." I tried to reassure her, desperate to remove the look of fear from her face. I couldn't stand it if

Cherie feared me. She wasn't afraid of anything. I focussed hard on myself and reached for calm, stroking the smooth soul stone in my pocket as I did so. I saw my hands gradually return to my regular colour, with only a faint red-brown tinge and a hint of swirling colours visible beneath my skin. I let out a huge sigh of relief and looked at Cherie again. She was still looking at me with mistrust. It was the look I had seen her cast over her mum's new boyfriends.

"Look, it's me, okay? Your best friend. We've been besties since the first day of school when you pushed Tommy Whitlock over for calling me a hippy kid! I know I look weird but it's still me here."

She smiled faintly and I reached for more memories, sharing moments of our friendship with her until she passed a hand over her sweat-stained face and put her hands up in mock defeat.

"Okay, okay, enough with the sentimental trip down memory lane. I get it. But what the heck happened to you and how did we get…" She looked around in confusion "…here? Last thing I remember, you were going to soccer camp on the mainland."

Shame filled me, and I felt myself blush. "Umm… I'm so sorry about everything that's happened to you because of me," I said in a rush.

Cherie frowned.

I took a slow breath. "Listen, I'm not sure what you remember, so let me start at the beginning and tell you everything. I never want to lie to you again."

As the sun set around us in a spectacle of glorious pinks and oranges, I laid the whole story out for Cherie, right up until the moment the gods spat me back into the world. I held nothing back, not even my confused feelings for Carlos and Indigo or the way I'd deceived her to get rid of her. A lot of emotions flitted over Cherie's face as I talked, but she heard me out in silence. I was worried she'd hate for me the way I'd manipulated her with my power, but she surprised me.

"Wow. You've been keeping a lot under your hood, babe. No wonder you look so stressed, with all these crazy people out to control you. First, let's sort out this little love triangle you've got yourself tangled up in, shall we?" She shook herself and looked around.

"We also really need to get the heck out of this desert and find a decent burger and a swimming pool. I've never been to Australia before, but I hear they have lots of that sort of thing." She smiled at me and took my arm, and we started walking in the direction the sun had set: two girls out for a stroll on a starlit night, talking about boys. Nothing could be more normal.

HERE ENDS BOOK ONE of Between Heaven and Earth

ABOUT THE AUTHOR

Julia Lindesay is the author of *The Wind's Kiss*, an exciting new romantic fantasy novel for young adults and those that are young at heart. She lives in Auckland, New Zealand with her family.

Connect on line
www.julialindesay.com